DENISE LEWIS PATRICK

Finding Someplace

SQUARE
FISH

Christy Ottaviano Books

HENRY HOLT AND COMPANY · NEW YORK

SQUARE
FISH

An Imprint of Macmillan
175 Fifth Avenue
New York, NY 10010
mackids.com

Square Fish and the Square Fish logo are trademarks of Macmillan and are
used by Henry Holt and Company, LLC under license from Macmillan.

Our books may be purchased in bulk for promotional, educational,
or business use. Please contact your local bookseller or the
Macmillan Corporate and Premium Sales Department at (800) 221-7945
ext. 5442 or by e-mail at MacmillanSpecialMarkets@macmillan.com.

Library of Congress Cataloging-in-Publication Data

Patrick, Denise Lewis.
Finding someplace / Denise Lewis Patrick.
pages cm
Summary: The weekend she turns thirteen, aspiring clothing
designer Teresa "Reesie" Boone is separated from her family
by Hurricane Katrina but, during the horrific storm and its
aftermath, begins to find strength in herself.
ISBN 978-1-250-07982-4 (paperback)   ISBN 978-1-62779-423-7 (ebook)
[1. Hurricane Katrina, 2005—Fiction.   2. Family life—Louisiana—
New Orleans—Fiction.   3. African Americans—Fiction.
4. New Orleans (La.)—Fiction.]   I. Title.
PZ7.P2747Fin 2015   [Fic]—dc23   2015000561

Originally published in the United States by Christy Ottaviano Books/
Henry Holt and Company, LLC
First Square Fish Edition: 2016
Book designed by Anna Booth
Square Fish logo designed by Filomena Tuosto

1   3   5   7   9   10   8   6   4   2

AR: 4.6 / LEXILE: 680L

For my aunt Elizabeth Lewis Smith—
a forever example of strength, courage, and resilience

PART ONE

Home

Chapter One

Reesie slammed the car door shut and stepped into the heat and heartbeat that was New Orleans on a summer afternoon.

"Hurry up! We can make the light!" her older brother, Junior, shouted.

"Oh, your brother is crazy, girl!" Ayanna giggled, grabbing Reesie's hand. The two girls looked both ways on the busy avenue.

"Be careful," Reesie's mother warned from the driver's side window, watching them run to the neutral ground with Junior. The light did change, so they stopped on the grassy strip that ran between the uptown and downtown sides of Canal Street.

Reesie was breathless. This shopping trip was for a

pair of special sneakers, and the sneakers were for *her*. Junior had offered to buy the purple-and-red canvas high-tops as an early birthday present. She'd be thirteen next week. A teenager for real, finally! And even though her parents said she'd have to wait for a big blowout birthday party till she was sixteen, Reesie was still going to rock a special outfit at her family birthday celebration this weekend.

"These sneakers are just what I need to pull off my birthday look!" she whispered to her best friend. "I can't believe Junior is being so nice to me."

Ayanna shook her head. "I can't believe you sew your own clothes, and they look so *good*!"

Reesie smiled with pride. She might have to wear boring uniforms to school, but she made up for them everywhere else.

"Check out that top!" Ayanna nudged her, and Reesie turned, but she only got a glimpse of the woman's shirt before the dark green St. Charles streetcar rattled past, blocking her view.

"I missed it." Reesie sighed, but her eyes were drawn in another direction. "Ayanna, those sandals! Look!"

The girls slowed down behind a group of tourists speaking loudly in German and carrying lots of souvenir bags. A tall woman in the group was tottering on the highest wedges they'd ever seen—and they were totally see-through.

"Am I looking at goldfish in those heels? For real, goldfish?" Junior moaned.

Reesie laughed. "They're fake fish, Junior. Fake!" She opened the door to the store, and cold air conditioning pulled them in.

"Okay, make this quick," Junior reminded them as they cruised toward the women's shoes. "Remember, after I pay for your sneakers, I have to go pick up my last summer check."

Reesie and Ayanna both nodded. So they only tried on three pairs of shoes each, and argued for only twenty minutes in front of the solid Ts. Reesie lost her argument that she could turn a size 2X T-shirt into a dress cool enough for her friend to wear in public. Before they went to meet Junior, who was waving wildly outside the front window, the girls posed together in the full-length mirror.

Reesie broke into a wide gap-toothed smile and smoothed her hair into a ponytail. She was chocolate brown and skinny, but had muscular arms and legs because she played softball. Her mom always said it was a good thing she was learning to make her own clothes, because fitting those shoulders would be a headache.

5

Ayanna, two inches shorter, shook her curly hair and made a funny face at her friend. In kindergarten they had pinkie sworn that they'd be sisters-from-another-mother forever. Seven years later they still hung out nearly every day.

Reesie's neon purple cell phone buzzed while they walked through the French Quarter with Junior. She looked down to see that it was Orlando, the third best friend forever in their trio, who they'd picked up around second grade. Up until the past year they'd all been inseparable, but things had gotten kind of weird lately. Orlando still texted Reesie at least once a day, but he spent all his free time working at his uncle Jimmy's restaurant. It almost seemed like he wanted to avoid being with her and Ayanna in person.

Reesie didn't take the call. She was a little mad at him for not joining their shopping trip. He said he had to work, but Reesie was getting tired of that excuse.

"I'm hungry," she said to Ayanna.

Even though it was only midmorning, jazz music floated from somewhere nearby, refusing to be drowned out by plain old street noise. The girls couldn't keep themselves from moving to the beats as they bounced along the narrow sidewalks, dodging vacationing families and tour groups in matching shirts.

As they neared the end of Canal Street, the flags of Woldenberg Riverfront Park flapped against the blue sky.

"I smell food!" Reesie said.

Junior rolled his eyes. "Anywhere in New Orleans, people smell food, Reesie." He dug into his pockets and pulled out a few wrinkled bills. "Y'all go on, get something to eat. I'll head over to the convention center to get my paycheck. Meet you back at Jackson Square in about forty-five, okay?"

"Wow! Sneakers *and* lunch!" Reesie smiled. "Thanks, Junior!"

"No problem," he threw over his shoulder as he rushed away. He would be going back to college in another couple of days, and she would miss him. But why tell him that?

"I'm sure going to miss your brother!" Ayanna said, pulling Reesie along.

"You're reading my mind again." Reesie laughed. "How about we get some beignets?"

Reesie loved the fluffy square donuts smothered in powdered sugar that were served at the famous Café Du Monde in the French Quarter. Sure, it was always packed with tourists, but she still remembered the very first time Ma Maw, her father's mother, had taken her there.

She'd been about three, and her legs had dangled only halfway down from the cast-iron patio chairs.

Anything that reminded her of her grandmother was nice these days. Ma Maw had died two years ago, but Reesie still found it hard to believe she was gone forever. She wasn't very good at missing people.

The girls took their time, stopping to look at what different street vendors had for sale, always keeping an eye out for some outstanding fashion trend. The line at the café was ridiculously short, and Ayanna snagged a table while Reesie got a plate of beignets and two bottles of water.

"We could pretend to be tourists too," she said, leaning toward Ayanna as she sat down. Ayanna shook her head and tilted it to the left.

Reesie caught on that her friend was listening in on the conversation at the next table.

"And so they say that New Orleens—she is just like Los Angeles! Waiting for the 'big one' to hit!" A man with a heavy accent was waving his arms in the air while the others at his table gasped and chattered in a language the girls didn't recognize.

Big One? Reesie mouthed to Ayanna, her eyes wide.

"Hurricanes and earthquakes," Ayanna whispered.

"I believe it is the hurricane season now," he went on.

"These tour guides, they never tell us anything. I saw on the Weather Channel that there is a hurricane, maybe right now, attacking Florida!" He pushed back in his chair, glancing at Reesie and Ayanna.

Reesie only shook her head and took a huge bite out of her beignet.

"I think that guy is what they call *alarmist*," Ayanna said, turning to watch the group stroll away, the man still going on about disasters.

Reesie shrugged. "He's right about one thing: it *is* hurricane season. But all New Orleans is waiting for is August 29. My birthday!"

Ayanna laughed so hard, she almost choked and had to swig her water.

"Yeah, you right, Reesie!" she shouted.

And everyone in the café who was a New Orleans native laughed with them.

Chapter Two

Three days later Reesie swirled in front of the full-length mirror in her bedroom, chanting out loud.

"All right, it's all riiight!" she sang along with John Legend and looked over her shoulder as she spun. The hem she had pinned in her flouncy bouncy skirt was perfectly straight. She stopped for a minute and smiled, touching the hot-pink thread she'd carefully zigzag-stitched down each seam.

She had rushed right in from school, and now was almost finished taking her birthday fashion design from a crazy idea in her head to the real deal. She had sketched the skirt, saved her allowance to buy enough purple denim, and then cut a pattern out of old *Times-Picayune* newspapers. Ma Maw would have been proud.

Ma Maw was the only grandparent Reesie had ever known—both of her mother's folks had died before Reesie was born, and so had her dad's dad. She and Ma Maw used to spend every day together before Reesie had gone to school, and afternoons once she'd started first grade. They'd shared laughs and stories and a passion for clothes.

Ma Maw had shown her how to sew a doll's dress when she was seven, and Reesie had been hooked. So when Ma Maw passed away, Reesie took over her sewing machine. The soft purring of the motor always seemed to bring Ma Maw back home, at least for a little while.

As Reesie danced to her sewing table, she tripped on the remote control, and the blast of a local newscaster's voice jumped out from her TV. The five-o'clock news! Junior had been in her room again. Why couldn't he watch TV in the family room?

She reached to shut it off, and suddenly heard a noise that wasn't part of her thumping music or the news broadcast.

"Teresa!" Her mother must have been knocking for a minute. She had skipped "Reesie" already and gone on to "Teresa." Reesie scrambled to open the door before she was called by her entire name: Teresa Arielle Boone. That would mean trouble with a capital *T*.

"Yes, Mama?"

Her mother was wearing her green nurse's scrubs with an old apron tied over them. She must've come right in from work and started cooking. The smell of onions and garlic and chicken floating from the kitchen made Reesie's mouth water. She realized that she'd been so focused on her sewing that she'd skipped her usual after-school apple slices dipped in peanut butter.

"I've got dinner going, so I'm going to take a shower. You can make the salad and—" Her mother stopped in the middle of her directions as she noticed Reesie's skirt.

"Oooh!" Her tone changed. "You've finished? Turn around! Let me see!"

Reesie spun on her toes.

"She finished it?" Junior yelled from the family room. Reesie had to admit to herself that it was actually kind of cool to have a brother who was genuinely interested in her life. She smiled.

Mama folded her arms and nodded. "Ma Maw would be proud of you," she said. "You'll look sharp on your birthday. I've already called Miss Martine to order your cake."

"Let me get a picture with my phone!" Junior crowded their mother out of the doorway.

Reesie made a face at him.

"Tell her to make nice, Mom!" he said.

"Reesie, Boo, make nice. I'm going into the shower."

Reesie faked an attitude after her mother left the room. "Junior, do *not* take any pictures. I still have to hem it. Can't you wait?" She slammed her door.

"*Project Runway* can't wait!" Junior sang to her from the other side. "You're gonna be the first designer from New Orleans to take the prize, girl!"

Reesie changed back into shorts and carefully hung up her skirt. For a minute she imagined that Ma Maw would be there next Saturday at her party. Ma Maw, alive again to see Reesie's first design. Alive again to see her turn thirteen. Reesie flicked the light off on the sewing machine before going out to the kitchen.

From the counter she had a view of her brother draped across the sofa in the family room. He was shoving handfuls of potato chips into his mouth and watching TV.

"You eat too much junk," she said.

Junior looked over his shoulder and mumbled, "What?"

Reesie dug into the fridge for cucumbers. "I said, 'Don't you miss my famous salad when you're up at Tech?' "

"Yeah, right." Junior laughed. Then he said, "Yo, Reesie, you know I'm leaving tomorrow to go back to school. I might not be able to come home next weekend, okay?"

Reesie pouted and ripped a head of lettuce apart.

"So you'll miss my birthday? Oh, I see." She sounded playful, but she was a little hurt. Junior could make a party *live*!

"Hold up! I have swim drills. Not my fault!" He was trying to apologize, but he'd picked the wrong way to do it.

"You're dropping me for that *swim team*?" Reesie furiously tore lettuce. She absolutely hated swimming and swimming pools, because when she was five, she'd slipped and fallen into a public pool. Her mother dove in right away to get her, but Reesie had been terrified of that kind of water ever since. She took showers, not baths.

"Sorry! Sorry!" Junior threw his hands up.

Reesie changed the subject. "Okay, fine. So how come you keep going into my room, switching my TV channels?"

"Because I'm trying to see what's up with this latest storm. As usual nobody around here is paying attention. Remember last year? When the mayor told folks to be ready to evacuate with some cash in their pockets?"

Reesie stopped slicing tomatoes, remembering the tourists' conversation at Café Du Monde. It *was* hurricane season, and this *was* New Orleans. Every summer they had to live with the threats of these wild storms churning themselves up into monsters full of wind and rain. The weather people gave them friendly sounding names like Andrew or Betsy. What real friend would come through and destroy your home the way a hurricane did?

"Not too many people left town," she said, thinking of how Ayanna's family had packed their car and driven north to Shreveport for a few days while the Boone family stayed put.

"That's what I'm talking about!" Junior said. "And you know the Weather Channel is saying—"

"A bunch of malarkey is what they're saying!" All at once their father came stomping into the kitchen, his policeman's handcuffs clinking at his side.

Reesie rolled her eyes at Junior, and together they mouthed along with his next words.

"No storm is gonna run *me* out! I'm New Orleans, born and bred!" He raised his eyebrows in mock surprise. "Y'all are laughing at your daddy?"

They both were.

"Our children have no respect for their elders, Lloyd!" their mother joked, coming to kiss their father hello.

"No respect." Their father laughed, slipping around their mother to take a peek into one of the pots on the stove. Reesie grinned as she picked up her knife again.

"I've got tons of respect for you, Dad, but I kinda respect hurricanes a lot more!" Junior said. He leaned across the counter to snatch a chunk of cucumber.

"How did we get on the subject of the hurricane?" Mama asked.

"Junior's obsessed," Reesie said, frowning as her mother threw another handful of sprouts into the salad bowl.

"Everybody is getting worked up for nothing," Daddy said.

"Lloyd, it's not nothing. We still have to prepare for what might happen!"

"We'll put plywood over the windows so they won't get blown in, pull all the outdoor stuff inside. That's just common sense." Daddy nodded. "A storm is no reason to get hysterical." He looked at Junior.

Reesie smiled, but her mother shook her head. Jean Parker had never gotten used to hurricanes. She'd come from New Jersey to go to nursing school, and she met Lloyd Boone at a football game. She always told her kids that she fell in love with him and with New Orleans in that order.

"Mama, you know you're just freaked out because there aren't any hurricanes in Newark!" Reesie said.

"That's not entirely true, Reesie," Mama said. "And, Junior, set the table!"

"Jeannie, this Katrina is still just a tropical storm," Daddy said. "It hasn't even been upgraded to hurricane status." He lifted the salad bowl. "And y'all don't forget—hurricanes change direction in a heartbeat. It could go off into the ocean somewhere."

Junior clanked knives and forks onto the table. "So I guess no evacuation for Sarge Boone. You don't believe in the *e* word, do you, Dad?"

"Right now the only place I'm going is to the dinner table."

"Good idea," Mama said. "Let's let this subject rest."

They sat down together. Reesie thought that was a great idea; she'd rather talk about getting ready for her birthday instead of some old storm.

"Daddy! I finished my skirt—"

"Reesie—" her mother interrupted. "Say grace, please."

"Bless this food, and bless the sun so it shines hard on my birthday this weekend! And I hope that Sergeant 'Superman' Boone is right about *this* storm!"

Reesie's father winked at her.

"Amen!" her mother said firmly. She smiled at Reesie and squeezed her hand.

Daddy nodded his approval and reached for the platter.

"You might be a teenager next week," Junior said, "but you'll be my little sister *forever*! Come on now, Reesie Girl. Pass the rice. I'm starving!"

Chapter Three

"*Ladies and gentlemen, the designer of the year, Teresa Arielle Boone!*"

The crowd went wild. Reesie was on the runway, and it was her own fashion show. Her shiny black hair was bone-straight and swinging, just like the short red skirt of her glittery spaghetti-strap dress. News cameras were flashing and digital cams were clicking. She was surrounded by models wearing the clothes she'd designed; Ayanna and Orlando were going crazy in the front row; and all the folks in the house were chanting her name.

"*Reeee-see! Reee-see!*" *She was grinning and loving the excitement. The audience got louder. She blew them kisses.*

"*Reesie!*" *She looked out and saw her parents. She waved but then felt a funny sensation around her ankles. Water was lapping over her toes. She looked out at the people, and they were all gone. She was alone, and she was surrounded by water.*

⚜

Reesie woke up shaking. It was always water in her dreams. She tossed and turned but couldn't fall back to sleep. The sun hadn't even started to glow behind the vertical blinds, but she was now wide-awake. She heard her parents' voices.

Usually, when both of her parents left for work so early, they drank coffee and whispered while Reesie peacefully slept. Not this time. They were arguing, something that almost never happened. She pulled her knees up in the dark and sat against her pillows.

"And in every storm scare," her mother said, "you get called in to work overtime, triple time. . . . What if *we* need you?"

In just four days the tropical storm that Junior had been so obsessed with had turned into a bona fide hurricane. Already Katrina had hit Florida like a monster, and the weather reports were screaming that she was headed right for the Gulf Coast, possibly New Orleans.

"Jeannie, be fair. I'm a police officer. It's my job!"

"It doesn't have to be." Her mother lowered her voice.

Reesie leaned forward, straining to hear more. The kitchen cabinet doors and fridge slammed open and closed.

"You could retire right now. You and Reesie and I could go together, just for a few days, to get out of harm's way."

"It's Reesie that I'm doing this for, Jeannie. You know that!"

"Shhh!" Mama hushed him.

There was a long pause. All Reesie could hear was the hum of the central air-conditioning unit outside her window. How was *she* in the middle of the drama? She wanted to know, but at the same time she didn't.

This was supposed to be the perfect birthday weekend. She'd had it all planned: later this morning was her hair appointment, then Ayanna was coming over for a preview of the birthday outfit. Sunday would be her special dinner. And there would be her neighbor Miss Martine's lip-smacking coconut cake. But now it seemed like the universe just wasn't going to cooperate.

She heard chair legs scrape against the kitchen floor.

"Jeannie, baby, I know you worry over me and the job. I promise, soon as I bank a little bit more for Reesie's college—"

"Lloyd, we're okay with that!" her mother said.

So that was it. Reesie felt a little guilty, as if she were making trouble for her folks. Her mother went on, sounding calmer. "I'm just anxious. It's everything they're predicting about *this* storm."

"Listen," Daddy said, "if it eases your mind, I'll call Pete on my way to the station and have him take Reesie back to Baton Rouge with them tomorrow. She can stay over with them a few days. Missin' some school in the first weeks won't set her back at all."

"I guess . . ." Her mother's voice trailed off.

Reesie settled back onto her sheets. Uncle Pete was her father's brother. He was also her *parraine*—her godfather. He was really cool and really laid-back. So was his wife, Tee Charmaine. Staying with them would make it feel like her birthday lasted extra long.

"I'm just not convinced it's gonna be that kind of dangerous, Jeannie. But I promise I'll call Pete . . . and next week we'll seriously talk retirement." The front door clicked open. "Everything will be all right."

"If you say so, Superman. Be safe out there," Mama said.

"Yeah, I will. See ya, baby." Daddy left.

Reesie pulled the covers up around her neck. "No more drama! No more drama!" she whispered to her pillow. Soon she was snoring.

When she woke up again, she blinked at the green numbers on her alarm clock. It was noon already, and she had a one-o'clock appointment at Bernice's Beauty Nest and Nail Salon! There was no time to eat. No time for TV. She jumped out of bed and tossed on a white T and denim shorts.

A trip to Bernice's could mean a couple of hours under the hair dryer, so she grabbed the backpack with her sketch pad and pencils in it and hurried out.

On the way, she thought about calling to tell Ayanna about her parents' fight. Ayanna would say that parents never agreed on anything—relax. And it would take Ayanna an hour to say all that. Instead Reesie texted, **HAIR@1. TALK L8R.**

The street was calm and quiet, and the air was already muggy and uncomfortable. She walked faster, looking up. The sun was out, no clouds in sight. No sign of any storm of doom. It seemed like a perfectly normal summer day. But then she remembered the crazy dream she'd had—*that* scene had started out perfectly normal too.

"Don't try and kick up on *my* birthday, Katrina!" she shouted out loud to the sky, not noticing until too late that Miss M, the same Miss Martine who was baking her birthday cake, was half hidden between the leaves of her giant tomato plants three houses away. She was frowning.

"Child, you better watch what you say!" Miss Martine bellowed, raising her bushy white eyebrows over her gold cat-eye glasses. She was wearing pink eye shadow and black eyeliner, and her ruby red lips were puckered with disapproval.

Reesie had nowhere to hide, so she waved.

Miss Martine had on her afternoon wig, a short and curly silver 'do with streaks of black. She wore store-bought hair and makeup like she was performing on a stage every night, but it was her desserts that were practically world famous. Peach cobblers, banana puddings, pies . . . and her cakes! Anybody in the Ninth Ward would tell you that Miss Martine Simon could just *look* at food and it would taste good. Her coconut cakes made it to every birthday, wedding, or picnic in the neighborhood.

Miss Martine shook a gardening spade as Reesie came closer to the edge of her yard.

"I know you think you're grown, with your birthday coming up, becoming a teenager and all."

"Yes, ma'am. I mean, no, ma'am!"

"And I know Lloyd and Jeannie Boone didn't raise you to play with the Lord like that!"

Reesie slowed down. "Miss Martine, I wasn't—"

"Teresa Boone!"

Reesie halted completely to show respect. The glaring sun was beating down onto her head, making her scalp sweat. Her hair situation was getting desperate, and Miss Martine was winding up for a sermon!

Miss Martine snatched her glasses off for extra effect. "Child, don't you know you're blessed?"

"Yes, ma'am." Reesie blinked at the bright reflection of the glittery beaded eyeglass chain.

"Tell your mother the cake will be ready around eight in the morning. And you better remember one more thing. . . . Don't you go trying to give orders to the man upstairs!" Miss Martine turned away, carefully tying her tall tomato plants to sturdy wood stakes.

"I won't!" Reesie answered automatically, and started walking again. Old people always took things totally the wrong way, she thought. Miss Martine must just be worried that her garden might be demolished by any strong winds. Reesie decided that maybe when she came home, she would offer to help.

Her cell phone buzzed to announce a text. She looked down quickly to read Orlando's message: **GT TXS L8R. CU.**

Reesie wrinkled her nose. *Going to Texas later. See*

you. What was he talking about? Uncle Jimmy's Blue Moon Café was one of the hottest places in town. He *never* closed his business, not even on Christmas Day.

She quickly texted back: **WHEN?** But there was no immediate buzz with his answer. She didn't have much time, but she needed to stop by Blue Moon to check this out. With any luck, Bernice was running late as usual. Kicking high and forgetting the heat, she sprinted three blocks and rounded a corner, bursting into the swinging door of Blue Moon. There was no bustling lunch crowd lined up at the register or elbowing up to the counter. Blue Moon, featured on Channel Three last month as the hottest neighborhood food joint, had exactly four customers.

Chapter Four

Reesie slipped into a window booth to catch her breath. The air conditioning blasted like an icy wind. Across the small dining room, Orlando was taking orders from a table where the only four customers were seated. She settled back to watch him, her urgent hair appointment fading to the back of her mind.

Orlando had worked at his uncle's place since he was ten. At first he had just cleaned up, but he'd turned thirteen already and now he was training to be a waiter. His shoulders looked muscular in a navy polo—Blue Moon's uniform—and his wavy hair was braided into a skinny rattail. Uncle Jimmy had warned him to cut it, but Orlando just flashed that bright white grin. And he did have eyes that crinkled when he laughed, like he was doing right now with the customers. Reesie blinked. Why was she thinking about Orlando like he was a *boy*? He was just Orlando. His knees were knobby and his feet were big, and . . .

Suddenly he looked up at her.

"Peanut Butter!" Orlando yelled across the dining room, and started in her direction.

Reesie cut her eyes at him and sucked her teeth. How could anybody think he was cute? *Well, you just kind of did*, she told herself.

"Why do you embarrass me like that, calling me by that second-grade nickname in public?" she asked as Orlando made it to her table.

"How come you didn't answer my text?" He had on some kind of cologne. Orlando was trying to be manly!

"I did! Besides, I was going to get my hair done." Reesie smoothed her ponytail.

Orlando leaned on the back of the booth across from her. "You know, we do killer po' boys here, but we don't do hair," he said with a grin. "You hungry?"

He pulled out his order pad and pretended to write, because Uncle Jimmy's narrowed eyes were aimed at the back of Orlando's head.

"For your information, no." Reesie used her most

snooty voice. She wanted to ask him why he hadn't been in touch for two days. She wanted to ask if going to Texas meant he'd forgotten all about her birthday party. But when the kitchen door swung open and she caught the aroma of a shrimp po' boy, her stomach gurgled, demanding food.

"Okay, okay. A po' boy," she said. "But make it fast. Remember, I have an appointment!" She felt silly for running all the way over, so she quickly added, "And what is this craziness about going to Texas?"

"We're tryin' to get outta the way of Katrina, that's what!" he said. He sat down, looking serious and very grown-up. Maybe that was what was weird about him lately—Orlando had turned thirteen first. Did he want to leave his old friends behind? Reesie wiggled in her seat and dropped her eyes away from his, playing with sugar packets.

"I know I'm gonna miss your birthday thing," he said. "I'm surprised your folks are lettin' you stay here! This could be the storm to wash New Orleans clear away!"

Reesie leaned across the table. He remembered!

"But this is *home*," she said. "For real, your uncle Jimmy is *evacuating*?" She looked across the dining room. The stools at the back counter were empty and the countertop was cleared of the usual cakes and pies in glass domes. Instead of the normal pandemonium coming from the kitchen, all she heard was the hum of a radio.

Orlando's gaze followed hers. "Yeah. Uncle Jimmy is closing up as soon as these customers finish. He's not even doing the Saturday night rush. He's gonna pick up Dré, Leila, and her kids, then we're taking the Escalade to Houston."

Reesie stared at him. Dré and Leila were Orlando's older brother and sister. That meant his entire family was leaving town.

"But the storm might change direction!"

Orlando shook his head hard. "Not Katrina, they say. Go on, call your daddy and get confirmation on the information. Ask him!"

Reesie hesitated. "You know I can't call him when he's on duty, not unless it's an emergency."

"Seems like an emergency to me," Orlando said, slowly rising from the table. "One shrimp po' boy comin' up."

"Extra mayo, okay?" Reesie said to the yellow crescent on Orlando's back. She couldn't call her father, but Junior would do. She took out her phone and dialed his number.

"Reesie!" Junior sounded as if he'd been running. "Can't talk now—just did laps and heading to the showers. Are you watching the Weather Channel? It was blowin' up before I left the dorm! What are y'all doing?"

"Doing?" Reesie felt Junior said the word like he meant *Duhh. Aren't you smarter than this?* She tried to answer with confidence.

"Mama and I are going back to Baton Rouge with Parraine and Tee Charmaine tomorrow."

"Finally! Mom got Daddy to be sensible and evacuate! Good. Great. Hey, gotta go. I sort of have a date. I'm really sorry about missing your birthday. I'll come the first weekend I can, okay? Bye!"

Reesie's insides fluttered. She looked outside. Three cars cruised by, packed with people and their stuff. They were heading for the St. Claude Avenue Bridge, which ran across the canal separating the Lower Ninth Ward from downtown, uptown, and highways out of the city. Reesie hit speed dial.

"Mama?"

"Hey, Reesie . . . this hospital is a madhouse. Is your hair done?"

"No, but I was talking to Junior—"

"Oops! Sorry, I have to go. I'm doing another shift because so many folks didn't come in today. So I won't make it home tonight, and—oh! I'm being paged. I'll call you back later."

"Wait!" Reesie's squeak echoed across the empty space. The other customers had left. She could hear Orlando and his uncle in the kitchen.

How could they laugh if the situation was really so serious? Reesie slowly slipped her phone back in her pocket.

Carrying a serving tray, Orlando swung open the kitchen door and began weaving his way toward Reesie. He carefully put her setup on the table in silence: silverware rolled up neatly in a blue paper napkin. Then, with a sweep of his other arm, he put the plate in front of her.

The zing of the spicy cornmeal coating on the shrimp made Reesie's eyes water, and she blinked, not wanting Orlando to think she was crying. Still, water leaked down her cheeks, and she had to wipe her face with the back of her hand.

"I saw you on the phone. You called your daddy?" he asked. "This ain't no joke, right?"

"No." She'd answered both questions at once. Orlando stood over her with his peach fuzz mustache. He seemed different. More like a man, somehow. She wasn't sure she liked that.

"How come?" she asked him quietly.

Orlando looked puzzled. "How come what?"

"How come this whole Katrina thing is so wild?"

Orlando's shoulders dropped, and his man face disappeared. Reesie saw little boy fear in his eyes for the first time in forever.

"I 'on't know, Peanut Butter," he said, suddenly turning away from her. "I'll call you when we get to Houston, all right?"

Reesie wanted him to come back. She wanted to say that she'd be in Baton Rouge, but she didn't say anything. She would text him tonight or in the morning. Instead she picked up the po' boy and took a huge too-big bite.

The sandwich tasted like cardboard. *Something's wrong with the world for true*, she thought. She hurried up, dropped a five on the table, and slipped away from Blue Moon.

Chapter Five

Bernice's Beauty Nest was packed with women and girls, all apparently trying to get their hair hooked up before they left town. Reesie sighed, realizing that she had forfeited her appointment. She slipped into a chair near the door anyway, and picked up a copy of *Black Hairstyles* magazine.

The four hair dryers ran constantly, and even with a window air conditioner plus two floor fans, the heat was almost unbearable. Within a few minutes Reesie heard so much gossip about the storm that she felt her head might explode. Luckily, Bernice's sister, Clarice, pointed to a free shampoo sink and waved Reesie over.

"Well, I'm not leavin' my livelihood!" Bernice announced to the room. She clicked her curling iron.

Reesie watched it sizzle over a teenager's waxed-stiff hair.

Reesie slouched in her chair as Clarice freed her hair from the scrunchie and let a loud rush of warm water pour over her head.

"What's your daddy sayin', Reesie?" Bernice called across the red linoleum floor.

"Aw, Bernice! The child can't hear you over this water!" Clarice shouted back. Reesie didn't let on that she could. And by the time her hair was washed and the rollers were in, no one seemed to be talking about the hurricane anymore. Bernice was waving a jumbo curling iron at a loud blond woman and talking her down that no New Jersey casino could beat a New Orleans riverboat casino.

"They don't have the mighty Mississippi up there, no!" Bernice made her point by clattering the curler into the heating unit. Everyone laughed. No one seemed to be upset, or even anxious.

Reesie hurried to sit under a hair dryer and pulled out her drawing pad and pencil so no one would ask her opinion again. She had been to New Jersey visiting family so many times that it wasn't any big deal. It was an okay place—mainly because it was close to New York—but Bernice was right: no place was like New Orleans.

35

Reesie busied herself by sketching outfits: the runway dress from her dream, a short wrap skirt with wide stripes, a jacket with a hood and backpack attached. Once her hair was dry, Clarice took out the rollers and trimmed a little off her ends, then combed Reesie's hair out carefully.

It was nearly six o'clock in the evening when Reesie stepped out of the salon with beautiful bouncing hair. As humid as it was, the air outside was a welcome change from the heavy perfume of hair oils and sprays floating inside the salon.

She texted Ayanna: **WRU?** and noticed a steady stream of traffic on the street. She'd never seen so many people from the neighborhood leaving when a storm was headed to town.

When she turned onto her block, she saw the Kerrys' van pulled crazily across their front yard next door, its back wide open. They were all out there loudly discussing what they should or shouldn't take, but they didn't speak to Reesie or even notice her. For a moment she wondered what would happen if everybody left.

She fumbled at her front door lock.

Inside her house the familiar smell of sweet cut roses mingling with the faint whiff of onions relaxed her the way it always did. As she tossed her keys onto a table, she saw that the red light of the answering machine was strobing. She turned it on, dropped into her favorite chair, and ran her hand around the cushion for the TV remote while she listened.

"Reesie!" The first message was from her *parraine*. "Hey, it's *Unc*. Lloyd is all over my case 'bout takin' you back tomorrow. What time we havin' this birthday thing? 'Cause the Saints are playin'!" *Click*.

Reesie laughed. She guessed that Tee Charmaine had cut him off. But Parraine didn't sound worried or hurried. She turned on the TV. The meteorologist was waving frantically as a giant orange-and-white swirl rolled toward the boot-shaped state of Louisiana on her map. Reesie muted the sound while the next message played.

"Reesie! It's Ayanna. I tried to get you on your cell. We're on the road! Mama decided to drive all the way over to her cousin Pam in Atlanta. Remember you met her and her son, Dante, last summer? Let me give you their number. It's—" Her voice was drowned out by a long loud beep. Reesie sat at the edge of the chair. Ayanna's voice came back.

"Dang! Oh! Yes, Mama, I know it's two steps away from cussing. I'm sorry. Where's the number? Here, Reesie. It's 404-555-1083. Put it in your contact list right now, okay? My battery's dying. Gotta go."

Ayanna's message had barely ended when the land-line rang, and the suddenness made Reesie jump. She leaned to look at the caller ID. It was her mother.

"Hello?" she answered breathlessly.

"Reesie! We're getting ready to move some of the patients out of the hospital, so—"

"What?" Reesie shouted, and then dropped her voice. "What's going on?"

"We're evacuating patients. I'm not sure where I'll end up, so I'm overruling your daddy and canceling the party. I'm sorry, honey. But I want you to go to Pete's first thing in the morning. I've tried to reach him, but the line is constantly busy. You text him and ask him to come early. Let me know when you speak to him, all right?"

"Okay." Reesie shivered a little.

"Good, good. I'll call again as soon as I can," her mother said. "Love you." Then she hung up.

"Love you too," Reesie said to the silence. She picked up her phone and wandered into her bedroom, trying to make sense of all the calls and conversations. Absentmindedly, she turned on the TV there, too, for-getting the house rule about saving electricity. She plopped onto her bed.

Somebody was talking about Katrina on every chan-nel she scrolled past: either people were running away from her, or they were nailing plywood over their windows and doors, daring her to keep out. Reesie dialed Parraine's number and was surprised when he picked up right away.

"Hey, girl, why've you been burnin' up your phone minutes trying to call me?" he asked.

Reesie struggled to keep her answer calm and casual. "Change of plans for tomorrow. Mama's stuck at work. She says can you come by for me in the morning?"

"Yeah, for sure," he said. "But what about your birthday?"

She sighed, glancing at her new skirt hanging on the closet door. "I'll celebrate next weekend, I guess."

"We'll be down there 'round noon. Tell your mama."

"Okay, Parraine. Bye." Reesie sent her mother a text: **GOT UNC.**

Then all of her energy drained away. She curled up on her bed and picked up her remote, flicking until she found one of her old favorite cartoon channels. She zoned out, watching one show, then another and another—anything to keep herself from wondering what tomorrow would bring.

Chapter Six

The mayor of New Orleans was whispering in Reesie's ear. She sat up suddenly. No, he wasn't—she'd left the TV on all night. Light was peeking through her blinds, and Mayor Ray Nagin was on the television screen.

"This is a threat that we've never faced before," he was saying. The people surrounding him on the screen were grim-faced, and even the governor of Louisiana was wide-eyed.

"The first choice is for every citizen to figure out a way to leave the city."

"Dang!" Reesie blurted aloud, but she was sort of relieved that she already had her own plans made. She squinted at the time on her clock. She hopped up and changed her slept-in clothes for jeans and the yellow baby-doll shirt she'd made last summer. Where was that Army backpack that Parraine had given her? She could jam lots more stuff in it. She lay across her bed to reach between it and the wall. Dust bunnies hopped up into her nose, and she sneezed just as her fingers grasped the webbed strap.

She tripped over clothes as she grabbed random items. First her black-and-green-striped notebook from the bedside table, along with her favorite fine-tipped marker. Keeping it moving, she made a quick pass through the bathroom, stuffing her Quick Sheen hair oil, soft brush, wrap pins, and lip gloss into the backpack. The lip gloss made her think of her toothbrush, which she hurriedly wrapped in a paper towel.

The landline started ringing.

Reesie ran into the living room, but the call had already gone to the answering machine. It was Miss Martine. Reesie had completely forgotten that she was supposed to pick up her cake—and that she'd promised herself yesterday she would help Miss M in her garden.

"Teresa? Are you there? What about your cake?"

Miss Martine had never sounded *old* like that before. She stood as straight as a six-foot-tall post, drove her own

Cadillac, and had even mowed her own grass until Daddy made Junior start doing it. But listening to her now, Reesie realized she must be up there in age. Ma Maw's face flashed in Reesie's mind. Miss Martine was at least as old as her grandmother would've been.

She snatched the receiver up. "Yes, ma'am! I'm coming, and I can help you get your yard things inside!" she heard herself saying. "I'll be over in a few minutes."

She ran back through the house, shutting off light switches, lowering the thermostat on the air conditioner. She gave the contents of her backpack one last check.

Somebody was knocking on the front door. "Who in the world could that be?" she wondered aloud, jerking the door open impatiently.

"Orlando?" Reesie shouted, then wished she hadn't. But Orlando didn't seem to notice that, or the drizzle that started falling. He shifted from one foot to the other with his hands shoved deep into the pockets of his cargo shorts. She could tell something was wrong.

"I thought you'd be in Texas by now!"

"We can't find Dré. I had to talk Uncle Jimmy down from leaving his butt behind. Girl, Jimmy is *heated*! Have you seen André?" Orlando's words ran together fast, the way they always did when he was upset.

Reesie shook her head. "No." Dré had always been

loveable, but always trouble. Still, he and Orlando were close brothers.

"Dang!" Orlando ducked his head. "Sorry, Peanut Butter . . . Your daddy isn't here, is he?" A flicker of a smile played on his face, but it quickly disappeared. "It's just that Jimmy says he's leaving in thirty minutes, Dré or no. Now that Nagin put out that mandatory evacuation order, all the highways are one-way outta here."

"For real?" Reesie's heart pounded.

"Yeah. You could come with us, Reesie!" Orlando said, looking hopeful. But she shook her head, telling herself there was no need to panic yet.

"No, thanks. Parraine is coming to get me."

"You sure?"

She nodded. "Yeah."

"Well . . ." He moved to leave, his hands still in his pockets. But then he turned back quickly and kissed her right on her mouth.

Reesie went numb from her brain down. She just froze, feeling Orlando's warm, wet lips pressed against hers. She felt like they stood there for thirty minutes!

But in thirty seconds, Orlando was easing away.

"Bye," Reesie whispered.

"Don't say 'bye,' say 'later,' Peanut Butter," he called

without looking back. He sprinted off. Reesie had to remember to breathe.

"Later!" she croaked after him. "Hope you find Dré!" Her head was spinning—and somebody was singing. For a minute she forgot the wide open door and the sharp raindrops pelting in. Then the ringtone of her cell finally penetrated her brain.

"Reesie!"

"Parraine!"

"The state troopers are sayin' the highway is closed southbound. They're not lettin' folks on. I'm gonna try a back way, but traffic is ridiculous. Keep your phone on. . . ."

Reesie snapped fully back to reality sometime after the word *highway*.

"Parraine, do you have room for somebody else?"

"Girl! Who?"

"Miss Martine, the lady who lives—"

"The coconut cake lady? If she brings one of those cakes, I got room!"

"Thanks! Thanks! Can you pick us up by her house? I'll lock everything over here."

"All right. Wait—Charmaine is tryin' to take the phone. . . ." In a second her aunt was speaking.

"Reesie? Don't try to bring everything you own, hear? Only the really important things."

"Okay. Bye!" Reesie was about to swing her backpack onto her shoulders when she thought about what Tee Charmaine had said. She remembered that her mother kept a brown envelope on her closet shelf marked IMPORTANT PAPERS. Reesie knew that birth certificates and stuff to do with their house were in it.

She immediately went into her parents' room. For a minute she hesitated—it felt weird going into their private space without permission. But what if the hurricane was really bad? What if they needed something in that envelope? She opened the closet door and found it easily. She carefully slid the envelope into her backpack, picked up her house keys, and stopped at the mirror by the door.

"I can't believe it took a *hurricane* for Orlando to kiss me," she told her mirror self.

She replayed the moment inside her head, smiling, and then her eyes focused on the scattered arrangement of pictures on the hall table. In the middle was Ma Maw, smiling and hugging Daddy when he'd gotten some promotion or another. Reesie impulsively picked it up, frame and all, and took a minute to zip it into her backpack. It was a nice old memory to go along with this sweet new one.

"I'll be back," she said to the memory-filled room reflected in the mirror. "Sooner than you think!" Then she grabbed one of Junior's caps off the hat rack by the door and slammed out.

Chapter Seven

The drizzle was more annoying than it was wet, and she brushed it away from her face, wishing that the weather would make up its mind. She rapped hard on Miss Martine's screen door before she found the bell—on the opposite side from where it was supposed to be. Loud old-fashioned chimes sounded somewhere inside. The door opened instantly, as if Miss Martine had been waiting right behind it.

"Here I am!" Reesie said a little too loudly. She suddenly felt nervous.

"Well, good. I'm not *deaf*, you know!" Miss Martine snapped, unlatching the screen. She seemed like her usual bossy, barking self again. Reesie relaxed. At least one thing was normal today.

"I'm sorry," she apologized. "I can only stay till my *parraine* comes to pick me up. He said you can come to Baton Rouge with us, and—"

Miss Martine sniffed. "I heard that Nagin on the radio. I'm not going anywhere. I'm just trying to clear up outside. And if you can help me move a few of my precious things in here away from the windows, in case they blow in, I'd appreciate it. Last year a plain old thunderstorm took the kitchen window right out!"

"Sure, I can do that." Reesie smiled.

"Well, step on in and rest your bag on the sofa."

A freshly baked cake smell tickled her nose; a crackly radio voice was droning on from somewhere in the back. She'd never been into Miss Martine's house before. When you ordered a cake, she met you at the door with it. Sometimes she chatted from her lawn chair on the stoop, or from the garden, like she'd done yesterday. Reesie had always been kind of curious to see inside.

But Miss Martine shoved an old pair of work gloves at her. "Now, I need to bring in my peppers and begonias, and all the potted plants first," she said.

Reesie nodded. She slipped her backpack off, tucking her ponytail up and tugging the cap more tightly onto her head. She really didn't like yard work, but that wasn't the point, was it? She followed Miss Martine back outside. There was a lull in the drizzle. Miss Martine was already carrying potted flowers around the side of the house.

"You can bring those folding chairs to the shed," she called over her shoulder.

"Yes, ma'am." Reesie snapped the two woven plastic lawn chairs shut and picked them up. She wanted to say that the shed might not be such a good idea. Daddy said it was always the shaky little toolsheds and carports that crumpled first.

But to Reesie's surprise, Miss Martine's shed was a solid little brick house, complete with a tiny window and a red painted door. The old lady stopped to pull out a key from one of her many pockets.

"Wow," Reesie said. "Your shed is fancier than some of the houses around here!"

Miss Martine laughed. "I know. André built it for me. It was one of his shop class projects."

Reesie's mouth dropped open in surprise. "André Knight? Dré?"

"Why, yes." Miss M arranged her plants in a row on a rough wooden bench just inside the shed doorway. "I knew his mother. He spent a lot of time with me after she passed away."

"I didn't know that . . . and I didn't know he could

do anything like this." Reesie ran her hand along the neat wall of bricks.

"I guess you know the younger boy better," Miss Martine said, turning around.

"Oh, uh, Orlando?" Reesie felt herself blushing. She wanted to change the subject, and fast. "Yes, ma'am. Miss Martine, don't you want me to take in everything that's ready to pick in your garden?"

"That's a good idea," Miss Martine answered. "The cabbage and okra . . . I have some baskets here—"

"Already on it!" Reesie scooped up an empty basket and hurried out of the shed.

Around noon, Reesie was bent in the backyard between rows of pole beans when her phone buzzed. She plopped the half-filled basket on the ground.

WHERE R U? It was her mother.

MS. M she tapped back. There was no immediate response. She tried dialing, but her call went directly to voice mail.

"Teresa!" Miss Martine called out from the kitchen window. "That's enough, in this heat! Come cool off and have some lemonade!"

"Yes, ma'am!" The drizzle had turned into light rain, and Reesie felt her shoulders aching as she lugged the beans toward the screen door. Her stomach growled when she entered the kitchen, which was filled with the smells of vanilla and coconut.

"You might as well have a look at your birthday cake," Miss Martine said, motioning toward the Formica counter.

Reesie popped the tape on the lid of the large white box and lifted a corner. Three layers of coconut-topped goodness were nestled carefully inside. She took a deep sniff and couldn't resist swiping her finger along the edge of the cake. It was hers, wasn't it?

"Mmmm . . ." She smiled.

"Did you hear from your uncle yet?" Miss Martine was piling fried catfish on top of an open sandwich roll. "On the radio they're saying the mayor has all roads leading in one direction—*out*."

"Yes, that's what my *parraine* told me!" Reesie raised her voice over the running water as she washed her hands at the sink. "But he's trying to get here another way."

Miss Martine put the sandwich on her old-fashioned, chrome-edged kitchen table and opened the fridge to take out mayo and mustard. She looked at Reesie over the top of her cat-eye glasses as she sat down.

"I guess this Katrina's going to be more serious than we thought. If he can't get here, you might just have to wait it out with me."

Reesie bit into her sandwich and thought for a minute while she chewed. "Miss M, would you ever leave New Orleans?"

Miss Martine shrugged and poured lemonade. "I'm too old, don't have anywhere to go. Besides"—she blinked—"the one time I did leave town, things didn't turn out so well."

Reesie was surprised. For her whole lifetime, Miss Martine had always lived just up the street.

"What storm was it?" she asked, swirling the last bit of her sandwich in a puddle of ketchup. "Was it Camille, the one Daddy always talks about?"

Miss Martine shook her head. "It was a different kind of storm, child. Come on, I have some pictures that will show you what I mean."

Reesie took her time gulping down the last of her lemonade. She wasn't into looking at pictures of the past—except for clothes. But Ma Maw had always gotten on her for not caring enough about *people* history. She eased her phone out to text Orlando.

FND DRE?

NAH. WRU?

@MS M. She had never texted Miss Martine's name before today, so she hoped Orlando was using his whole brain.

TM2H! Too much to handle? What was he talking about? After all his flakiness lately, he had texted to let her know he was evacuating. Then he had come to ask her about Dré. And then that kiss! Why hadn't he explained himself?

Did it mean what she thought it might mean? Ayanna was always talking about kids at school who were "more than friends." Was that what was happening with Orlando? Reesie really wished that she could talk to him now, live and in person.

She stared at the tiny screen, but she didn't call. And she didn't text, either. *Neither did he*, she told herself, slipping her phone back into her pocket.

"Teresa?" Miss Martine was calling her.

"Coming!" Reesie answered, hurrying up from the table. When she stepped into the shadowy dining room, her feet sank down into the thick shag carpet. She eased around the huge table, bumping into one of the heavy thronelike chairs.

The dining room opened through a curved arch into the living room, where Miss Martine had stopped. Reesie stood in the arch, blinking as her eyes adjusted to the dimness.

There were books everywhere: piled on top of two faded velvet sofas and balanced on small dark tables.

Behind the sofas, tall bookcases stretched up to touch the low ceiling; through their glass doors Reesie saw paperbacks jammed next to expensive-looking leather-bound volumes with gold letters on their spines.

Miss Martine flipped on a fancy brass table lamp, and the space was suddenly glowing. Every inch of the living room's wall space was covered in frames. Reesie gasped and moved closer.

There were yellowed flyers from shows on Bourbon and Rampart Streets, dated sixty years ago. She saw programs from plays at New York's Broadway theaters. There were wild old movie posters and black-and-white photos of people dressed to kill.

"Wow! This is like a museum!" Reesie stopped to read the autograph scrawled across the bottom of one photo.

Teenie, write a song for me sometime! Love, Louis. Reesie's brain registered the man's round face and wide grin. She spun around.

"Louis Armstrong! You *knew* Louis Armstrong, Miss M?"

"Child, I've known lots of people."

Reesie turned back to the picture to check out Louis Armstrong standing with his arm around a tall curvy-bodied young woman. She wore her wavy hair parted down the middle and slicked close to her head. Her dress draped low across her chest and flowed into a tight fit at the hips, with a scissor-pleated edge on the skirt. Thrown across her wide shoulders was a plump dark fur that seemed to have both an animal's tail and head attached to it. The woman was smiling wide, and she had dark full lips.

Those lips were the same as Miss Martine's ruby red mouth.

"But this is you!"

"It's me."

"And you're wearing a killer dress, and a *fur*!"

"Called a stone marten," Miss Martine said.

"Were you a singer?" Reesie tried to wrap her mind around Miss Martine and this long-ago glamorous life.

"Let's say that I didn't always make cakes. Here." Miss Martine held out a small red book. Reesie dropped her eyes to the fading silver print on the leather cover.

Woman Everlasting . . . Poetry and Stories by Martine Odette Simon, 1949. Reesie looked up at her neighbor in wonder. "Miss M! You're famous!"

Chapter Eight

"No, no." Miss Martine gave Reesie a half smile. "I only wanted to be a writer. But none of my family even finished grade school, and they didn't think much of my trying to be different. I wanted to go to college. When I left that house on South Roman Street, I knew I wouldn't ever go back. I decided to run off to New York."

"So that was your storm, huh?" Reesie perched on a fluffy velvet stool. "You left home to make your dreams come true."

Reesie wondered what it would be like if she got the chance to fly all over the world, walk the runways, and see herself and her designs in magazines. That was her dream, but she couldn't quite picture leaving her family behind. She couldn't imagine them not backing her up, either.

"I met other colored writers—black, y'all say now— up there. They were people who treated me like family. . . ." Miss Martine's voice trailed off, and her eyes became distant.

"And you got a chance to write your book!" Reesie said.

"I got lots of chances." Miss Martine nodded. "I tried writing for the movies too. Believe it or not, there were black folks making movies back then. The Johnson brothers, and Oscar Micheaux." Miss Martine paused to laugh at Reesie's blank expression. "He was . . . uh . . . the Spike Lee of my day," she explained. "Oscar liked one of my stories, gave me a piece of money for it. Not much. Then he went and made a movie that wasn't anything like it. I got invited to the opening anyway. That was his last film."

Movie scenes swirled in Reesie's mind, first visions of the way-out dresses and evening gowns the women in the old black-and-white movies wore, then the fabulous clothes actresses wore on TV awards shows.

"Did you get to walk the red carpet?" She gasped. "Was your dress custom designed? Oh, oh! And did you wear that—that fur from your picture—what was it? A rock martin?"

Miss Martine laughed out loud and then looked thoughtfully at Reesie, pulling on her cat-eye glasses as if she wanted to get a good look for the first time.

Reesie froze, afraid she'd somehow said the wrong thing.

"A stone marten. And we seem to be going on and on about *me*," Miss Martine finally said. "Tell me about what *you* do."

"What? I just go to school and stuff."

"What is *stuff*? I don't believe at all that you keep your head on your studies every single minute. You are too lively for that!"

Reesie didn't know how to answer. Miss Martine was somebody who'd been famous and had hung out with stars. Surely, she wouldn't care about an almost-teenager's dream to be a fashion designer! Reesie nervously fingered the edge of her baby-doll shirt.

"Did you make that?" Miss Martine asked. And she didn't ask it like it was impossible, the way some of the kids or teachers at school did.

"Yes, ma'am."

Miss Martine came around and gently examined

Reesie's flat-felled shoulder seam, and the lace pieces she had sewn around the neckline.

"Appliqué!" Miss Martine murmured. "Child, you're good! Very good."

"Thanks," Reesie said proudly. "My Ma Maw taught me how to do it. Miss M—" A question burned at the back of Reesie's mind. "Do you mind if I ask you something?" Reesie hoped she wouldn't bring back bad memories; still, she had to *know*.

"Not at all," Miss Martine said, folding her arms across her chest. "It's been good talking about the past."

"Well . . . I guess I don't get how you—I mean anybody—could give up something you wanted so much! How could you give up writing? All that fame and everything?" Her voice faltered.

Miss Martine didn't react with anger. In fact, she looked a little sad.

"Oh, child. I wasn't ever famous! And anyhow, do you think this country was ready for anybody colored—trying to make a living off words—to be famous? I wrote my heart out. Yes, and got one book published. Never made much money off any of it. I stayed up North for a while, waiting for something big to happen. I went overseas after the war, where lots of colored artists and writers had done better. Wrote some more poetry and a few stories. Ran out of money, though. I ended up writing for love, and cooking for a living."

Reesie thought of Orlando for some crazy reason. She blushed and pushed him out of her mind.

Miss Martine seemed to pick up on it. "I don't mean a man, either! I mean, writing was what I wanted to do, what I loved. Cooking was what I *had* to do to earn my keep. I've been cooking ever since."

Reesie opened her mouth to ask what happened to the writing, when Aretha Franklin's voice belted out *"R-E-S-P-E-C-T,"* from her cell phone. She watched Miss Martine's eyebrows jump, and laughed. "It's my mom's ringtone," she explained.

"Teresa Arielle Boone!" Her mother's voice was shaking.

"Mama? I'm okay! Didn't you get my text? I'm at Miss Martine's—"

"Oh my God, honey, forget about the cake!" There was so much commotion in the background that Reesie could hardly hear, and her mother was practically yelling.

"Mama? Mama!" Frightened tears welled in the corners of Reesie's eyes.

Her mother took a deep breath. "Boo, I wish I had

followed my first mind and taken you away from here!" she said angrily. Reesie couldn't exactly tell who she was angry at, though.

"Look," her mother went on. "Parraine called me. Things are so crazy that there's no way he can get into the city to pick you up. I can't find your father. You stay where you are, you hear me? This hurricane is coming, it's coming in bad. I don't want you to get caught by yourself!"

Reesie swallowed. She was aware that Miss Martine was standing quietly in the doorway, listening.

"But, Mama." Reesie tried to sound calm. "I'm not *by* myself. I'm with Miss Martine!"

"Right. They don't expect the storm to make landfall until tomorrow morning, so your daddy will come for you. . . . Are you listening?"

Reesie was nodding without saying anything.

"Reesie! Teresa! Put Miss Simon on the phone!"

"I'm here. Yes, Mama. Just a minute—" A loud busy signal interrupted the conversation, and all at once her mother was gone. She tried redialing, but she got a busy signal, then a recorded message: *"We're sorry, but circuits are busy. Your call cannot be completed at this time."*

"Well, I guess I have company now, don't I?" Miss

Martine said. "If I know Lloyd Boone, he's going to find a way to get his baby girl. You can count on that."

Reesie wanted to say something, anything; but she was still dangerously close to crying. In her heart, she knew Daddy would do anything for her. He simply refused to believe anything would happen to his New Orleans—ever. He couldn't have known that the city would officially be shut down. Usually, when her parents agreed to disagree, everything worked out. But this time Katrina had jumped into the mix, and even Lloyd "Superman" Boone might not be able to make it right.

Chapter Nine

Reesie looked out Miss Martine's front window. Clouds had finally rolled in, and a strong, steady rain was falling. There were no more slamming doors, or cars creeping along. She didn't see headlights or taillights, or even house lights. It was hard to tell if she and Miss Martine were the last people on the block.

What were her parents doing, and why hadn't she heard from them? Was Orlando having room service somewhere? Was Ayanna hanging out with her cousins? She even smiled to herself at the thought that Bernice might still be finishing up one last customer.

Maybe it would all be a bust, but Reesie felt the weight of waiting, and it was horrible. Waiting for her phone to ring or buzz. Waiting for Katrina.

"Let's take our minds off all this storm mess," Miss Martine said, clapping her hands. "Child, when I'm upset, I cook. In fact, I bet I can *cook* up a bigger storm than old Katrina!"

Reesie couldn't help but burst into laughter.

"We'll make meat pies," Miss Martine told her. "That way, if the power goes out, we'll have something we can eat cold."

They proceeded to chop onions and garlic and bell peppers. Miss Martine directed Reesie to drawers and cabinets stocked with dishes, bowls, and fancy serving platters. Each one had a story, and Miss Martine told them all. Reesie found herself laughing even more and asking questions, forgetting the tight place in the pit of her stomach. She felt as if Ma Maw were with her again.

The aroma of the frying crust and spicy meat began to fill the house as the rain lashed hard against the windows. Reesie counted one, then two dozen of the golden half-moons spread on paper-towel-covered trays—and Miss Martine was still scooping more pies out of the hot oil.

"You know, I ran into a fellow once who was selling videotapes of Micheaux movies. I don't know where he found the film, but they're the real deal! I bought one or two of them. We can watch one if you set up the video machine. I never can figure that thing out."

"No way!" Reesie turned to see Miss Martine's eyes twinkling. "Black-and-white?"

"Course!" She nodded toward the other room. "Look through that armoire in front of the couch."

Reesie stared at the huge piece of furniture, and when she went to pull at its double doors, she found a bulky old TV set sitting on top of a VCR. Not even a DVD player. She smiled to herself. But then, the boxes stacked neatly beside the TV were all videotapes. She scanned the titles until she saw the name *Micheaux* written in spidery script on the spine of one box. The tape inside only had a plain label on it that read SWING, 1938.

"This is soooo old!" Reesie murmured. She slid the tape in, rewound it, and it was ready to go. "It's in, Miss Martine," she called out, pressing play.

"I'll be right there."

Just as Reesie settled onto the sofa, the lights flickered. Then the TV picture turned to static, and the power went completely out.

"Hey!" Reesie shouted.

"Good gracious! It's only the lights," Miss Martine said.

But Reesie jumped up, banged her knee, and sent something thudding to the floor.

"Don't move," Miss Martine ordered. "You'll hurt yourself. Let me get my searchlight."

"O-okay," Reesie answered. She wouldn't dare move. It was pitch-black. The wind was actually whistling, the way it did in horror movies, and trees were scratching at the windows. For a minute she imagined that she felt the whole house move, but then it seemed still.

"That's freaking crazy," she mumbled out loud.

"Say what?" A strong beam of light suddenly shone from the kitchen. Reesie could see Miss Martine's face in the shadows.

"N-nothing." Reesie was still trembling. And all at once, she was super-hungry. It was ridiculous. How could she be totally scared, and starving too?

Reesie blinked. Miss Martine was smiling, motioning in her direction.

"We might as well eat a little something," she said. "Seems to me, people always eat when their nerves are bad. Watch where you step, now."

Miss Martine plunked her flashlight on a counter and rifled through a kitchen drawer. She produced a tall candle, lit it, and set it in the center of the table.

"What kind of New Orleans girl are you, afraid of a little wind?" she asked.

Reesie shrugged. "One time during a storm, when I was little, Ma Maw took Junior and me into the middle bedroom while the house shook like crazy! I mean, we were okay and everything, but—I just don't like any of it."

"I've been blessed since I bought this house," Miss Martine said. "I never suffered more than a few inches of water and some missing shingles."

"But aren't you—weren't you scared to be in here by yourself?" Reesie asked.

Miss Martine smiled. "I know it's odd for you young people to be alone, but we old people get used to it."

Reesie did think it was weird, but she didn't say that. She nervously chewed on a meat pie, listening to the wind rumble. The rain was pounding now, and a clap of thunder almost knocked her off the stool she was sitting on. The searchlight was dancing along the counter by itself. The house was really shaking. The walls were straining and creaking.

"Miss M, do you think . . . do you think Katrina is the 'big one,' like everybody's saying?"

Before Miss Martine could answer, an explosive burst of wind blew the candle out and rocked the building from its brick foundation up. Glass rattled and windows popped, tinkling as their shards flew everywhere. Reesie jumped off the stool and crawled under the table. Miss Martine eased to her knees and grabbed one of Reesie's hands. Reesie squeezed the old lady's soft arm.

"Just keep still," Miss Martine whispered.

The searchlight finally clattered to the floor and went out, spinning underneath the table alongside them. Then a thunderous crash hit the side of the house.

"Wh-what was that?" Reesie's eyes were wide in the dark.

"I think it was the roof over my bedroom," Miss Martine said. A moment later they heard a sound like a giant shower running at full force.

Katrina raged and stomped across New Orleans.

Reesie and Miss Martine clung to each other under the table. The hurricane kept rolling. Reesie closed her eyes tight, telling herself that it couldn't possibly be *her* house that the trees were falling on. It couldn't be her house that the wind had just flattened with another *boom*.

"Now, I'm just thinking," Miss Martine said calmly during a lull in the wind. "How silly an old woman am I to stay here for a bunch of books and souvenirs from two lifetimes ago?" She shifted her weight away from Reesie and clicked her tongue, fussing at herself.

Distracted from her fear, Reesie opened her eyes.

"That's not silly. It's like you said. These are your precious things!"

"Things seem to be all I have left," Miss Martine said.

"I think there are some things that are special," Reesie said.

"Like what?" Miss Martine asked as trees crackled and cracked outside.

Reesie described the antique clock Mama's uncle had brought back from his time in World War II, and the Kenyan stool her parents had gotten when they went to Africa before she was born. She told Miss Martine about Junior's basketball trophies and her own stacks of sketchbooks. . . .

"And then there's Ma Maw's old sewing machine," she said.

"She's the one who taught you?"

Reesie nodded.

"I should have known. Your grandmother always had an eye for fashion. I made her a pie every now and then, and she'd hem a dress for me in return."

"That's so cool," Reesie said, thinking how crazy it was that she never knew any of that.

Rain whipped against the windows, pounding on the roof. For a moment the roar outside magnified the small noises inside: boxes bumped and shifted; windows rattled all around. It was like intense music, overwhelming with its sound and hypnotic rhythm. Reesie tapped her toe to the strange beat, and tried to imagine that she was somewhere else. Anywhere else.

⚜

Orlando was kissing her in Audubon Park, one of the most beautiful places in New Orleans. She was wearing a brilliant blue sundress that she'd designed. . . . But they were wrenched away from each other by some force she couldn't see. Next she was at the Audubon Zoo, sailing around on the carousel and looking frantically for the brown speck that would be Orlando, but she couldn't find him as the ride spun faster and faster.

"Hey! Open up! Open up! Let me in! Anybody in there?" Orlando was yelling. . . . How in the world could she let him *in* to the carousel? How loud could that boy get?

"Open *up!*"

Reesie jumped. She'd been asleep.

"Teresa!" Miss Martine was shaking her shoulder.

"Wake up, child, there's somebody at the door, and I'm too stiff to get up."

Reesie blinked awake. The wind had stopped.

Her back ached; her shoulders and legs ached. The door chimes were making her head ache. But before she moved, she looked at Miss Martine.

"What happened? Is the hurricane over?" Reesie knew that there was a calm spot in the middle of every hurricane, and as the storm passed over land, that eye in the center could fool you.

The doorbell chimes had been joined by furious banging.

"It's over," Miss Martine said. "Go on, now. See who it is!"

"We're in here!" Reesie shouted. "I'm coming!" Maybe it was her father, she thought. She moved a little faster, clumsily unbolting all Miss Martine's security locks and throwing the door open.

Standing there like a giant wet puppy with dreadlocks was Orlando's missing brother, André.

Chapter Ten

Reesie was so shocked and angry that she barely noticed her feet squishing into the carpet. "Where have *you* been?" Reesie frowned at him.

"Well, Reesie Boone," he drawled, "this ain't your house! What're you doin' here? And anyway, can't a brother come in and get hisself dry?"

Before Reesie could answer, Miss Martine spoke out.

"You watch that attitude, André Knight! This is *my* house!"

Dré's shoulders immediately shot from slumped to straight.

"Oh! Sorry 'bout that, Miss M. I just came by to check on you. . . ." Dré stepped in, and a girl appeared behind him.

She was tall and skinny, wearing crazy high platform heels and a tight white dress splashed with creamy flowers. She wore a scarf wrapped around her head like a turban, which Reesie thought was actually kind of cute, and glitter sparkled along with the water drops on her long fake eyelashes.

The pair slipped in the door quickly, but not before Reesie caught a glimpse outdoors. It was still raining, and all she could see was the top of a big tree that the wind must have blown down, and the wires of a split telephone pole snaking across the yard.

"Teresa, can you get those blinds open over there?" Miss Martine called to her.

Reesie knelt on the couch and let more of the weak light in. Then she pulled out her phone and tried her mother's number.

She was stunned when her mother picked up on the first ring.

"Mama!" Every muscle in Reesie's body relaxed.

"Reesie! Are you okay? Happy birthday, baby!"

Reesie swallowed hard. She was thirteen! She'd waited so long, expecting to feel special on this birthday. And now?

"Everything . . . all right . . . Miss Simon?" Her mother's words were drowned out by loud static.

"Yes, but—"

"Moved patients . . . Your father knows where you are. . . . Love you—" The signal was gone. Reesie took a deep breath and turned on Dré.

"Orlando was going crazy looking for you! Uncle Jimmy evacuated to Houston."

"I figured." Dré shrugged. "We went to the house yesterday, and they were all gone. I know Jimmy wasn't wastin' time lookin' for me."

"That's not true . . . ," Reesie began.

Dré waved her quiet. "I know my uncle, Reesie Boone. You don't!"

"Why is that any of her business?" the girl snapped. She shifted her body closer to Dré's. Reesie wanted to yell back that it wasn't *her* business either—but she pressed her lips shut tight.

"S'alright, boo," Dré said. "I've been knowin' Reesie Boone since she and my baby brother were crumb snatchers. We can tell her and Miss M." He grinned in the dim light.

"Tell us what?" Reesie asked.

"Me and Tree—Eritrea—we went and got married Friday. We've been celebrating for three days!"

"Married," Miss Martine repeated slowly.

"Married?" Reesie squealed. "But you're only nineteen, same as Junior! That's—that's—you're—"

"Yeah, *married*." Eritrea wiggled her long fingers in Reesie's direction. "See?" A slim silver band reflected the light from the window blinds.

"How could you do something like that without even telling your own brother?" Reesie demanded. "I wouldn't ever forgive Junior if he pulled a stunt like this!"

"I feel bad about it, 'cause Orlando's my boy. But Jimmy don't have no love for me. Nothin' I ever do is right for him!"

"We're the only family we need, right, baby?" Eritrea pulled Dré close and gave Reesie a look that dared her to say something.

"André!" Miss Martine spoke sharply, flicking on her flashlight. "That storm blew in part of the roof. Come on with me and look at it."

"Right, Miss M!" Dré quickly separated himself from Eritrea.

Reesie had always thought of Dré as funny and a little goofy. Junior had called him flaky when he dropped out of high school. But Orlando said Dré had gotten his GED and a steady job.

"You can't believe Dré has a wife, can you?" Eritrea whispered.

Reesie rolled her eyes. "I'm not even thinking about it," she lied, easing past Eritrea toward the short hall that led to the bedrooms.

"Well, I'll be! My poor house!" Miss Martine was saying. Reesie stopped so suddenly that Eritrea bumped into her.

"Watch out for the glass," Dré warned.

A tree limb had crashed through the roof and ceiling. Light rain was pattering through the leaves. Part of the tree had taken out the window near Miss Martine's bed, and landed on her chifforobe. The window glass had exploded into dozens of tiny fragments that were sprinkled over everything in the small room. Reesie's sneakers crunched on the floor.

"This is bad, Miss M," Dré murmured, shaking his locks.

Miss Martine didn't respond. She bent slowly to pick up some matted brown thing from the floor.

"Oh!" Reesie gasped. "Is that the stone marten from your Louis Armstrong picture?" The fur hung limply in Miss Martine's hand.

"Stone-what-you-say?" Eritrea tipped closer.

Reesie looked sadly at the wildly flowered dresses

spilling out of the smashed chifforobe. Their colors and dyes were already running together as they lay soaked across the floor and bed. She forced her eyes away. All that fantastic old-school fabric!

Dré crossed the wrecked room to take a closer look at the damaged roof.

"Seems like there ought not be so much water puddled in here," he said, crouching near the floor and making his way in slow motion around the room.

Reesie realized that he was right—every move they made squelched into the rug.

"It's from the roof, right?" she asked.

He shook his head, looking puzzled. "Let me take a look outside."

"It's only a little high water," Eritrea chimed in.

Reesie saw Miss Martine's worried face as they headed back into the living room.

"I don't know 'bout that," Dré muttered. He opened the front door, and fast-moving water rushed in. Reesie was almost thrown off her feet by the quickness of it. Dré tried to push the door shut, but the force of the water was too strong.

"Help me!" he shouted. Eritrea waded in his direction, and Reesie pulled herself along the edge of the couch toward him. The three of them put all their combined weight against the door. Slowly, it moved. Dré clicked the lock and looked over his shoulder at Miss Martine.

"This ain't only 'a little water,' Miss M. The water's rising, and rising fast. We should go up into your crawl space."

Eritrea stared at him. "Are you crazy? Up in a nasty attic with *spiders* and stuff?"

Miss Martine frowned. "You don't think . . ." She let her words trail off. Dré started grabbing the pillows off the sofa, pushing them tightly against the bottom of the door. Reesie looked down. Water was already above their ankles.

"I don't know what to think, Miss M, 'cept that this is trouble with a capital *T*!"

Chapter Eleven

"Exactly what kind of trouble?" Reesie's voice didn't sound teenage to her own ears. It sounded small and scared.

"Trouble with the levee, Boone," Dré answered.

Reesie could only nod. She'd heard over and over in her junior-high Louisiana history classes that one of the things that made New Orleans special was the way most of the city was situated. The city's bowl-shaped land-scape was positioned between Lake Pontchartrain on the north end and the great Mississippi River on the south. The low land was protected by high banks of earth called *levees*. If the waters rose too high, or if the levees ever leaked, the city could be flooded.

"This water should be in the bathtub!" Eritrea was indignant.

"Yeah, well, bathtubs can overflow, can't they?" Dré said.

The water was already swirling around their calves. The pale carpet underneath looked like sand at a beach. The heat and heavy humidity in the house was sucking the air away, and Reesie's chest felt tight. What if she had to swim?

"Miss M, you got something like a crowbar or sledge-hammer?" Dré asked.

"Look in that hall closet!" Miss Martine had made her way into the kitchen. Dishes clinked and cabinet doors slammed shut.

Reesie looked at Dré as if he had lost his mind. "Why do you need that?"

"In case we need to chop our way out of the attic, Reesie Boone. Now come on, you and Tree help me get the attic ladder down."

"This is crazy," Eritrea murmured, shaking her head. She kicked off her heels. "We just got married!" Her voice was shaking. "This is supposed to be a special time. A happy time, right?"

"Yeah," Reesie said, strapping her backpack onto

her shoulders. "Special." As she started after Eritrea, something on the dining room table caught her eye—it was Miss Martine's book of poems. Without thinking, she picked it up to put it into the backpack. Then her eyes traveled up the wall to Louis Armstrong, and she swiped down his picture.

"Who's in that picture?" Eritrea asked curiously.

"It's just something special to Miss M," Reesie said. She knew she sounded rude, but she didn't feel like trying to explain. Mr. Louis Armstrong and *Woman Everlasting* were absolutely the last items that would fit before her bag burst at the seams.

Dré pulled one of the heavy dining room chairs into the hall so it was underneath the trapdoor in the ceiling that led to the crawl space.

Reesie and Eritrea held the chair steady so Dré could climb up to reach the latch. He yanked it, and a folding ladder slowly lowered itself. Eritrea grabbed the ladder and pulled while Dré jumped onto it.

"We'd better hurry," he said. "Miss M, come on!"

Miss Martine came into the hallway holding tightly to a small cooler and a plastic grocery bag.

"You go first," Dré insisted, taking the cooler and passing it to Eritrea. She pushed her way to the ladder next, barely giving Miss Martine's dripping slippers time to get halfway up.

"Hey, after you!" Reesie said, but Eritrea didn't seem to hear—or care. Dré grinned, and a little of his goofiness showed again.

"I still love her, you know?" he said.

Reesie scrambled onto the ladder. She didn't answer Dré and she didn't look down. To her relief, when her head poked into the attic, it wasn't completely dark. Slivers of light shone in through the vents in a small gable at one end. The space was already crowded with old suitcases, boxes, and empty picture frames.

"How come the roof isn't broken up here?" Reesie asked, trying to squeeze between Eritrea and a beat-up leather trunk.

"That part of the house was added on," Miss Martine said. "We should stay dry here."

"Lucky for us!" Dré finally huffed up the ladder, carrying the crowbar. His wild hair brushed against the rafters. Reesie could imagine spiderwebs . . . and spiders. She pulled her legs up and wrapped her arms around her knees.

"Found this in the closet, too!" He held up a small transistor radio. "So far I only got static, but maybe I can switch batteries from one of the flashlights and get it to work."

"Good thinking," Miss Martine said. "Teresa? Eritrea? Can you get any calls out on those cell phones?"

"Mine's dead," Eritrea said, shaking her head.

Reesie twisted her body and managed to pull her phone out. She squinted at the ghostly screen, which read: NO SERVICE AVAILABLE.

"How long do we have to stay up here, anyway?" Eritrea poked Dré with her elbow.

"Till the water goes down," he said.

Reesie crawled to the open trapdoor and blinked, looking down. The hallway had become almost too dim for her to make out anything, but the smell of wet furniture and curtains and clothes was already strong. Then she thought she saw a glimmer of water, and she jumped back onto her knees, scraping them on the rough floor.

"I—I think it's higher!" she whispered.

"Now, let's not panic," Miss Martine said. "What would you all be doing if we weren't stuck up in this musty old crawl space?" Her voice sounded a little too loud and a little too cheerful.

Dré cleared his throat and reached for Eritrea's hand. "Tree and me would be enjoying our happy new home!"

He aimed the beam of his flashlight right at Reesie. "And what about *you*, Boone?"

Reesie opened her mouth, ready to give him a sharp comeback. Instead tears stung her eyes, and a different answer forced itself into words.

"I'd be turning thirteen."

Chapter Twelve

"Happy birthday to ya! Happy birthday!" Dré did an awful imitation of Stevie Wonder's singing, making Tree giggle like a five-year-old. Reesie couldn't help smiling.

"Happy birthday, Teresa." Miss Martine gave Reesie's hand a tight squeeze.

She snapped open the plastic cooler. "Here. You have a birthday apple."

"Hey, can I get in on that, Miss M?" Dré asked. Miss Martine passed out apples and last night's cold meat pies. The attic began to smell more like a house than a cave.

Reesie sniffed away her tears, thankful that the others were munching so hungrily that they didn't seem to notice.

"I thought your big day was yesterday," Miss Martine

said. "And we left your cake down in the kitchen, poor thing!"

"Yeah, too bad we don't have that up here," Dré said.

Eritrea nodded in the direction of the ladder. "That cake is underwater by now."

"I can always make another cake," Miss Martine said soothingly. "I just feel so sorry that you have to spend your special day up in my attic, Teresa! I wish I could give you some kind of little birthday token."

"She already *has* something from you." Eritrea slurped on her apple. *How can she slurp on an apple?* Reesie wondered, fumbling to open her backpack.

"I thought you might want to save this. . . ." She couldn't bring herself to say, *In case you lost everything else*, so she just held out the photograph and the book.

Miss Martine leaned forward.

"How thoughtful! I insist that you keep *Woman Everlasting*. When this is all over, I'll autograph it for you. That'll be for your birthday, you hear?"

"But, Miss Martine, I didn't—"

"Hush now. Let me see if this old brain can recite some lines. It's been so long. Oh yes! The end of one poem went like this: 'Find someplace, / get yourself somewhere that you can always enter, / knowing you will be loved.'"

As Reesie listened, the rhythm and feeling of Miss

Martine's husky voice rose to the low rafters and bounced off them. She could imagine those words flowing out of the gable like the water flowing in beneath them. The last few words made her feel closer to all the people in the attic. Like they were family, as crazy as it seemed.

"That—that was deep," Dré said.

"Amazing." Reesie nodded.

"I mean, you could have written that yesterday," Eritrea said.

"Thank you." Miss Martine sighed. "It was a long time ago." She gently pressed the book back into Reesie's lap and sat still, as if the poetry had carried her off into a different world. Like she was remembering *her* someplace.

Minutes dragged into hours. Dré fiddled with the radio. Scratchy, screechy sounds filled the attic. He and Eritrea kept up a whispered, couples-only conversation. Miss Martine dozed. Reesie pressed herself close to the vent and strained to peek through the louvers. The slats were so close together that she couldn't see anything more than strips of weak sunlight. She pulled out her sketch pad and a drawing pencil anyway.

The shadow and light made a funny gray-and-white pattern on the page. She used it to design a clothing pattern. First she drew angular lines across the page, so that with the bars of light it looked like a crisscross. Then she made squiggly wavy lines, spaced unevenly. Water. Stupid water. She couldn't get away from it.

All at once, the radio crackled and a woman's voice came through clearly. Miss Martine jerked awake, knocking over the cooler.

"As of this hour, unconfirmed sources report that both the Seventeenth Street Canal and the Industrial Canal have breached. There's no official word on the extent of flooding so far, but some areas, such as the Lower Ninth Ward, may be experiencing up to four feet of floodwater. . . . Repeat, may be experiencing four or more feet of flooding from a suspected levee breach. . . ."

Reesie dropped her pencil. The edge of her sketch pad trembled against her knees.

"We're trapped up here!" she shouted.

"Dré?" This time Eritrea sounded like a little girl. Dré pushed past her to get to the ladder. Reesie held her breath as first his feet disappeared, then his knees. Just as his face vanished, they heard loud splashing. His head popped up again. When he crawled off the ladder, he was wet from the waist down. Reesie saw his eyes and knew how scared he was. Her heart thumped.

"We gotta get on the roof," he said, reaching for the crowbar. "Miss M, I'm sorry, but we have to bust it up."

"*What?*" both girls yelled at once.

"Calm it down, a'ight? Yeah, the roof. How else are we gonna get out of here?"

"The roof?" Even Miss Martine sounded uncertain.

Dré twisted his body to remove his shirt. Reesie stuffed her pad away, reminding herself that she wasn't a kid anymore. She was thirteen, and she was Sergeant Superman's daughter.

"Let me help," she said.

Dré looked over his shoulder at her. "Yeah, you right! I'll start it off."

"I'll hold the flashlight!" Eritrea said. The stream of light was shaking like her hand must have been, but Dré leaned and whispered something to her. The light steadied.

"Okay. Get back as far as ya'll can, now!" He tapped at the wood with the hooked end of the crowbar, then drew back and slammed hard. Nothing happened.

Tap, tap, *wham!* There was a creaking sound, like what Reesie had heard as Katrina passed over the house taking some of the roof with her.

"How long do you think it'll take?" Eritrea asked.

"Don't—know—" He panted. *Thump, bam! Bam!*

Reesie waited as long as she could before she shouted, "Dré, give it!" He stopped to wipe sweat from his eyes,

89

and she grabbed the crowbar. It was heavy in her hands. She wanted to swing the tool like a baseball bat, but there was no room. She balanced herself evenly on her knees.

"Close your eyes!" Dré said. "Give it all you got!"

Reesie rammed the crowbar straight up. *Bam!* She heard more cracking. She counted: two, four, six hits. Her shoulders ached.

"I'll take it, Boone." Dré gave Reesie a nod. "You did pretty good."

He didn't add *for a girl.* Reesie's opinion of Orlando's brother was undergoing a slow change. He took the same position he'd had before and rammed the crowbar into the shattering rafters.

Wham! Wham! Bang!

"Watch out!" he said. Eritrea's flashlight moved wildly, wood splintered, and a gust of air streamed in. They saw blue sky.

"We did it, Boone!" Dré wrapped his shirt around his hand and carefully pushed out as many jagged pieces of wood as he could from the edges of the hole they'd made.

"Let's pull that trunk over here so I can get a leg up," he said.

Reesie obeyed. She watched him flinch as he eased himself out. She wouldn't forget to tell Orlando that his big brother had turned into a hero.

"I never seen *anything* like this!" Dré shouted down at them. "I—whoahhhh!" There was a loud bump, then the sound of sliding, falling. . . . Reesie held her breath, waiting for an awful splash.

"André!" Miss Martine moved toward the trunk.

"Oh my God! Dré?" Eritrea started to climb up. In the light it was obvious she was terrified.

"I'm good!" He sounded breathless. "I slipped—it's somethin' treacherous out here! Y'all gotta be real careful."

Eritrea shook her head and gave Reesie a weak smile. "I can't let anything happen to him. André is all I got."

Miss Martine patted Eritrea on the shoulder. "Those Knight boys are hardheaded, child. Don't you worry. André's not going anywhere!"

Eritrea nodded and turned away, but not before Reesie saw her tearing up.

Dré's face loomed over them, blocking out the light. "From what I'm looking at, I think we better hurry up!"

Eritrea got up on the trunk first. "I'm not tall enough!" she said.

Reesie hurried to look around for something, anything else to use as an extra step. She spotted a plastic milk crate filled with junk, and quickly dumped it. She slapped it on top of the trunk and steadied it while Eritrea climbed up and looked out.

"What can you see out there?" Miss Martine asked.

"Oh, it's . . ." Eritrea hesitated, like she couldn't even find the right words. "It's just *bad*!" She ducked back in, shaking her head. "Everything is underwater." She wound her scarf around her waist and tied it. In seconds she was back atop the crate, so that half her body was outside. Pushing up on her elbows, she wiggled up and out.

"I got it. Next!" Eritrea looked down, her braids swinging.

"Okay, Miss Martine." Reesie nodded.

But Miss Martine gave Reesie a little push. "You go on first."

Reesie shook her head. "Oh no, ma'am! If my daddy ever found out that I left this attic before you, I'd be grounded for life!" She gave Miss Martine a little shove back. "You go."

Miss Martine slowly climbed onto the trunk. Dré and Eritrea reached down for her arms. They pulled and Reesie pushed until Miss Martine was sitting on the edge of the hole, her legs dangling. For a minute she seemed to be having a hard time catching her breath, but then she eased herself out. While the others got Miss Martine settled, Reesie collected the radio. She took the last meat pies out of the cooler and put them into the grocery bag.

When Dré finally called, "Ready?" Reesie handed everything up to him. She focused only on avoiding splinters as she lifted herself out. Eritrea caught her arm, and she felt a weird physical sensation when her Chucks touched the shingles, just like the one time she'd been on a skate ramp with Junior.

Reesie crept carefully toward a short metal pipe sticking out of the roof, eased her arm around it, and slowly looked around. She'd figured that once they were out of the tight house and even more cramped crawl space, she would feel relieved. She'd thought Dré was their rescue. But now, in the open air, in ninety-degree heat, she began to shiver.

What had happened to her neighborhood? Where were the front yards and the fences and the porches and chairs? Her stomach heaved. She'd lived here all her life, but nothing looked familiar. It was a river of rooftops and treetops. Telephone poles, thick as young trees, leaned every which way, trailing wires.

And it looked like the water was still coming.

"This is sure nuff some wicked mess," Dré said as the entire side of a house floated past.

Chairs and bicycles and other personal belongings followed, taken by the current of the floodwaters. Reesie could make out a colorful flat thing tangled in tree branches close by, and realized she was looking at the top of an SUV.

For a few long minutes nobody said another word.

"What do we do now?" Eritrea said. She and Miss Martine were huddled next to the old brick chimney on the slope of the roof, just below Reesie.

"We wait." Dré sighed. He sat with his legs dangling off the edge.

"My daddy knows where we are. He's coming," Reesie said. She'd always believed her father could do anything, but she was worried. It was already afternoon—sooner or later it would be dark. How could he possibly find Miss Martine's house then? What would happen to them if he didn't?

There was no rain. There were no cars, no crickets. No faint voices or pounding beats of speakers floated in the air. It felt as if the only life left in New Orleans was there, on top of this little house on Dauphine Street.

Miss Martine told them stories about New York, and tried to encourage them until her energy faded. Eritrea kept fiddling with the radio, but she couldn't get it to work again. Reesie had parked herself right at the peak of the roof so she was as far away from the water as she could get. She stared at the changing sky as the afternoon passed and the dusk started on its way.

"It's almost night," Reesie announced to no one in particular, flicking the flashlight on. Her birthday skirt was underwater. And Ma Maw's sewing machine and all the yards and yards of fabric stashed under the bed. Her lifetime collection of sketchbooks and markers. Junior's trophies. Her parents' African masks. Everything. Soaked. Ruined. Gone.

She kept wanting to hear sounds, sounds of anything—even the awful winds of Katrina would have been better than this, this nothingness. She didn't even want to close her eyes as exhaustion pulled them shut, because she feared what might happen while she slept.

Each time she nodded off, she jerked herself awake to stare at the strange shapes below, and at the blackness in the distance that should have been the bright lights of the lively French Quarter.

"Reesie! Reesie!" Eritrea was whispering. "Miss Simon! Listen!"

Reesie blinked into the dark, groping for her flashlight. She heard a faint humming.

"It's a boat! Turn on the flashlights!" Dré shouted. "Hey!"

They all started yelling.

"Help!"

"Over here!"

The putt-putting motor grew louder as the boat came closer. Water slapped at the side of the house in its wake. The motor stopped. Reesie aimed her light in the direction of the sound.

"How many of y'all up there?" a deep voice asked.

"Four!" Dré answered.

"We gotcha," the voice said calmly. "We gotcha."

PART TWO

Lost

Chapter Thirteen

"Thanks, man. I don't know how long we would've been stuck up there." Dré shook hands with the man piloting the wide flat fishing boat.

Reesie was glad to be off the roof, but held on tightly to the seat. She'd been on ferries before, but this was her first time in a small boat. It took her a minute to stop thinking about whatever might be out in the dark besides the black water.

"This is like another planet," Eritrea whispered, sitting beside her. "I hope they're taking us somewhere high and dry!"

The words from Miss Martine's poem popped into Reesie's head: *Everybody wants to find someplace.* Reesie leaned around Eritrea.

"Miss Martine?"

Miss Martine had been awfully quiet when the men helped her off the roof. Now, as Reesie looked, she saw that Miss M's face and her whole body seemed to be sagging.

"Miss Martine!"

"Mmmm . . ." Her eyes fluttered before she opened them wide. "I'm feeling a little weak, Teresa," she said, closing her eyes again.

"Dré! We have to do something!" Eritrea said.

Dré moved toward Miss M quickly, and she slumped against him. "Hey! They got doctors where we're going?" he asked.

The second man in the boat swung his bright light on them. "We can get you to the Saint Claude Bridge," he said. "They say the National Guard's pickin' up from there."

"Stay with me, Miss M." Dré shook Miss Martine's shoulder. "Come on now!"

Eritrea pulled a bottle of water from the bag they'd brought and tried to get Miss M to drink.

Reesie watched, paralyzed. Why was all this happening? Was it because she'd played with God, like Miss Martine had said? What if she had stopped to help Miss M that morning? Maybe then everything would be different. . . . She thought about Ma Maw. Her grand-mother had suddenly felt faint one day too; Daddy had rushed her to the emergency room. She never came home.

"Yo! We got a sick lady down here!" Dré was yelling.

Reesie saw the concrete of the bridge through dozens of dancing flashlight beams. The boat bumped gently against it, and Reesie got ready to climb up. Instead someone grabbed her arm and pulled her out. The water was only a couple of feet below the bridge rail.

She lay flat out on the hot wet asphalt, panting, and then sat up. Her eyes gradually adjusted to the moving lights, and she could see past the dozens of people stand-ing, sitting, or wandering around. There was a line of stalled cars and trucks down the center of the road. But the strangest, most frightening sight was the people who were still sitting in their boats down on the access ramp, where floodwaters had crept up and swallowed the road.

Reesie was shaking. The shaking was inside, and she couldn't do anything to stop it. So she counted to ten the way she did when Junior got on her last nerve. She reminded herself that she'd gotten this far not by herself, but with Dré and Eritrea and Miss Martine . . . Miss Martine! Reesie rose to her knees to look around. There was a small group of people crowded a few feet away.

Among them she spotted Eritrea's once-white dress. She seemed to be trying to get the people to back off.

"Hey, give her some air!"

Reesie made herself get up and walk over. "C'mon, move it, move it!" She used her best bossy voice, the way her father would have.

Eritrea raised her eyebrows, but smiled. "Your daddy's a cop, right?"

Reesie nodded and squatted down. Miss Martine was hardly breathing. There was a sheen of sweat around the edges of her wig. Her eyes fluttered, but stayed shut.

"What can we do?" Reesie sat back on her heels, feeling her heart racing.

Eritrea reached into the folds of her scarf and pulled out one more tiny bottle of water. She gently pressed it to Miss Martine's lips, but the woman wouldn't drink. She couldn't.

"She's gotta go to a hospital," Eritrea said, looking up. "Soon."

Reesie took a deep breath and looked around. Dré had melted into the pulsing crowd. Reesie craned her neck to look for his wild dreadlocks, but her gaze wandered away, beyond the bridge. The sky was turning pink. Sunrise.

Then she thought she heard a faint rumbling noise

coming from the other end of the bridge. There were so many people crowded together over there, more than she'd thought. Men and women were pacing, some smoking cigarettes and some debating loudly about what their next moves should be. Teenagers hung over the rails, and other women and children were huddled in clumps together. Some were crying, but many of their faces looked blank, like they weren't feeling anything.

Someone else noticed the sound and shouted, and all the bodies began to move.

"Trucks!"

"It's the National Guard!"

"Help!"

"Get us out of here!"

Towels and T-shirts and even a few diapers flapped in the air to signal for a rescue. Two huge vehicles rolled up, each with several uniformed soldiers on board. Reesie stood up. The strange trucks looked like something from a movie. The tires were almost as tall as a person. As the engines powered down, the people backed away. Some of the soldiers carried guns.

One soldier hopped down off the first truck. Just as his feet touched the ground, Reesie heard a familiar voice shout: "Hey! Hey, Mr. National Guard Man!" It was Dré.

"Sorry, man!" The guardsman motioned with his

hands for Dré to move back. He shouted over the noise, "We're picking up elderly only! Elders only!"

"Okay, it's our grandma, man! She's 'bout to die, or something! You gotta take her outta this madness, please, Mr. National Guard Man!"

Our grandma? Reesie shot a look at Eritrea.

"Here! Here she is, see?" Dré rushed to Miss Martine's side, pulling Reesie along.

"Work with me here, Reesie Boone," he said in a low voice. Reesie fixed her face to match Dré's lie. It wasn't hard. She *was* totally whacked out and very worried about Miss Martine.

The soldier bent to check Miss Martine's pulse, then he waved back at the trucks.

"All right. She goes," he said to Dré.

"She don't go nowhere without my sisters!" Dré pushed Reesie and Eritrea forward.

"Look, fella . . ." The guardsman sounded threatening. Dré didn't back down.

"Times is desperate, man," he said. "They gotta go with her, else she'll wake up all confused and take a bad turn!" The soldier tightened his jaw, but he'd made a decision. While other soldiers were moving through the crowd, he took the two-way radio from his hip and barked into it.

"I'm not going without you," Eritrea said in a low voice to Dré.

"Yes, you are, girl. I'll find you. You know I will!"

Reesie thought of Orlando. She looked away to give them time to say good-bye or something, when Dré grabbed her by the arm.

"Boone, you take care of Miss M. And you stick with Tree. I know your daddy is gonna find you, so she'll be okay too. A'ight?" He stared at her so hard that she blinked.

"O-okay! Okay."

"We've got other rescues to make!" the guardsman was yelling. "Then we're dropping at the Superdome. That's all I can guarantee!"

Dré gave a thumbs-up and helped the soldier make a chair with their arms. Reesie and Eritrea helped Miss Martine up. A second guardsman worked with them to lift Miss Martine up and into the chair. When Reesie and Eritrea followed, she was surprised to see that there were already people inside. Eritrea leaned around the green tarp to wave.

"Bodies inside the truck!" a soldier on the ground ordered.

"Hold on!" the driver shouted, and the truck began to back up.

Most of the people inside the truck were old, or mothers with very little kids. One tiny little girl stayed huddled in a ball underneath her mother's arm, her big eyes wide and unblinking.

How long before I see my *mother again?* Reesie wondered. She dropped her gaze to her sneakers. They were scuffed and muddy, and she was ashamed to be wearing them. Then she thought of how the rest of her must look—and smell. The jammed-together bodies around her stank of sweat and funk, food grease and baby oil and fear. *So must you, fashion diva wannabe,* she told herself.

Chapter Fourteen

A ride that should have taken twenty minutes took over an hour. Every few minutes, Reesie squeezed Miss Martine's hand and got a weak squeeze back. None of them were talking. The only sound was the swishing of water as the heavy truck lumbered toward downtown, or the shouting of soldiers when they had to stop to clear debris from the road.

Reesie decided to distract herself with her drawing pad. She eased her backpack off and immediately felt lighter, better. One of the kids across from her watched as she took out her pad and pencil. She flipped to a clean page and started to sketch a raincoat.

"Hey, that's good!" Eritrea said.

Reesie glanced up. The little kid's eyes were glued on her.

"Want to draw?" Reesie asked the boy. Without waiting for an answer, she carefully tore off several sheets of paper and passed them to him. Then she dug into the backpack, and her fingers touched her markers. For one second she hesitated, then she handed them over.

"Say thank you." The boy's mother shook his shoulder. He only grinned.

"It's okay." Reesie smiled.

"Yeah," an old voice said, "troubles bring folks together!"

"Mmm hmm . . . ," someone agreed.

"Look," Eritrea whispered, pointing outside. They were in the business district now, and the streets were deserted and dry. Soon they began to pass other National Guard trucks and soldiers on foot. The truck stopped.

"Good morning!" A guardswoman appeared, shouting directions. "This is the Superdome. It has been named an evacuation center by the mayor. All evacuees will get more instructions and help once you're on the ground. Careful getting out, and good luck to you!"

The passengers who could stumbled out of the truck. Two medics with stethoscopes hopped in. One carried a bag and a clipboard. A man with an oxygen tank got the first medic's attention. The other turned to Miss Martine, tossing Reesie the clipboard.

"Name? Age?"

Miss Martine couldn't get words out.

Reesie stuttered, "I—uh—"

"Martine Simon. Miss Martine Simon," Eritrea answered. "She's eighty."

"Write it down," the medic ordered. Reesie did. The medic looked up. "We'll take care of her. You can go."

"But—" Reesie said.

"Come on." Eritrea pulled her away.

"I told Dré I would watch out for her!"

"They got it. We need to watch out for *us*. Look at this!"

A week ago these streets had been filled with strolling tourists, busy summer workers, horse-drawn carriages, and lively strains of jazz. Now the scene was like a reporter's photo taken in some country at war. The plaza outside the dome was strewn with towels and blankets and belongings, and the people those things belonged to. Many people were old, some in wheelchairs. They were every race. There were groups that looked like families, and there were individuals set apart.

There was some kind of pain on every face.

"You think Miss M's going to be all right?" Reesie took another look back.

"André says she's a tough old lady. So, yeah."

Arm in arm, they navigated through the defeated-looking people whom the National Guard soldier had called *evacuees*. Reesie didn't like the way the word sounded. It wasn't a word to describe plain old Americans living in New Orleans.

Her eyes met the eyes of a roundheaded boy wearing a Saints T-shirt. He was clutching the hand of a man who looked just like him: his father, Reesie guessed. But though the little boy's big eyes followed Reesie and Eritrea as they passed, he didn't really seem to see them. He looked as if he were lost somewhere inside himself.

It occurred to her that she was lost too. She was an *evacuee* too.

They walked closer to one of the entrances. Reesie pulled a door open, and the stench made her gasp.

"Ugh! Smells like a bathroom!"

"We're not going in there." Eritrea shook her head and pulled Reesie away. They kept going, slowly wandering around the outside of the circular stadium. Nothing seemed to be happening; no one seemed to know what to do next. When a caravan of Red Cross trucks appeared on the street, there was a wave of movement.

"Food! They got food!" a shout rang out.

"They got any water?"

A swarm of people began to flow out of the Superdome. Reesie and Eritrea were suddenly surrounded and swept along with the mass of bodies.

"Maybe we can at least get something to eat," Eritrea whispered.

Reesie's stomach growled in agreement, but they were jostled and bumped along without any way to control themselves.

"Catch my hand," Eritrea said.

Someone shoved Reesie, and she tripped on the heels of the person in front of her. "Hey! Move along, or get outta the way!" someone else shouted.

Eritrea was jerked in the opposite direction. "Reesie!" Her voice was moving away.

"Tree!" Reesie threw her arms up over her head to keep from being trampled, and she tried to scramble to the outer edge of the crowd. Still, she was hustled and pushed even farther, until she was finally right up against the glass doors leading back into the lobby. To get away from the crush, she swung one of them open and stepped inside the building.

The Superdome was huge. Reesie had been here more than once, to football games and a concert or two. The lobby and corridor were brightly lit then, filled with vendors selling souvenirs and hungry people lined up at the concession stands. Now the corridor was littered with trash, and people hung around everywhere: behind the empty food stands, in the tunnels leading to the seats, and in the shadows. She could see their shapes moving, and every now and then there was the flash of a cigarette lighter, or the narrow line of a weak flashlight.

Reesie stayed in the angles of sunshine still coming in from the doors and floor-to-ceiling windows, keeping an eye out for Eritrea when she looked outside. At the entrance to one tunnel, she peeked to get a look at the stadium floor inside. She saw sunlight right over the football field, so she went closer.

People were camped out in the stadium seats, and people were sleeping on cots on the football field. The light was coming from a hole in the Superdome roof— Katrina must have blown part of it away. Reesie was stunned.

"Hey, what you got in that sack?" a rusty man-voice asked from close behind.

She started farther into the stadium, but got snatched back into the tunnel by the strap of her backpack.

"I bet you got something good in there."

Reesie instinctively began to wiggle out of the pack, trying not to look back.

But a hard hand gripped her shoulder and pulled her around.

"Stop! Stop!" She raised her voice, poking with her elbows as she got tangled in the straps. She saw his full face. It was hard to tell how old he was, but he had a stubbly beard and unkempt locks, and he reeked of beer and cigarettes.

"I bet you got a fancy expensive phone, too," he said, reaching for her pocket.

"Help! No!" she screamed, trying to throw her knee up against his chin. He'd already gotten ahold of her cell phone and yanked it out. She tried to remember everything Daddy had taught her to do—scream, fight back—but she could only be terrified.

"Hey! Get your hands off her!" It took Reesie a minute to register that the voice was Eritrea's.

"Mind your business," the man growled, but Reesie was able to pull away.

"She *is* my business! You get off her, or I swear—" Eritrea was running into the tunnel.

Reesie never knew where Eritrea reached to pull out the knife. She only remembered the gleaming silver of the open blade, the loud ripping of the backpack as the thief broke the strap, tearing away her sleeve with it, and the squeaking of his sneakers as he ran.

"He's got my phone!" Reesie cried out, flailing her arms. "He's got Miss Martine's book, and my sketches! He—he—he's . . . got . . ." She suddenly lost her voice. *All of my mama and daddy's important papers . . .*

Eritrea wrapped her in a tight hug. "You okay? You're okay. Just be still for a minute. You're okay, right?"

Reesie couldn't have moved even if she wanted to. She wasn't okay.

"I shouldn't have come in—you said don't—"

"Reesie—"

"Please. I was so stupid! D-don't tell Dré, don't tell anybody," she whispered, looking straight at Eritrea.

Eritrea took a deep breath. "It's yours to tell."

Reesie nodded slowly. What she wanted to do was forget—forget this, forget Miss Martine getting sick, forget the flood and Katrina.

"Let's get some air," Eritrea said, keeping her arm around Reesie's shoulders.

Reesie felt like she was moving in slow motion while

the rest of the world was normal. *But none of this is normal*, she thought, shaking her head. She kept shaking her head.

"Boone!" From far away, Reesie heard her name. She wasn't even sure if what she'd heard was real.

"Boone! You here, Teresa Boone? Looking for a Teresa . . . Arielle . . . Boone!"

"That cop is calling you, Reesie! Look!" Eritrea tapped Reesie's arm. Reesie focused on the uniform, but she didn't recognize the young, curly-haired officer.

"Over here! This is Reesie—she's Teresa Boone!" Eritrea waved.

"Well! Teresa Boone, your daddy, Officer Lloyd Boone, is lookin' all over New Orleans for you."

Superman. Reesie smiled nervously, but she couldn't let herself believe it, not yet.

"*My* daddy?"

"Yeah." The officer pointed over his shoulder. "He's right over there by that Humvee." Reesie saw him, talking on a police radio. He looked up at her.

The crowd parted, the clouds parted, and Reesie buried the last two days deep inside. She took one look at Eritrea and then walked as steadily as she could. She was determined to act like the same old Reesie.

"Daddy!" her voice squeaked out. "What took you so long?"

"Reesie Bear!" He lifted her completely off the ground, pressing her to his heart and holding her as if he would never let her go again.

"Daddy," she whispered, and then sobbed.

Chapter Fifteen

Reesie didn't wonder how her father had managed to commandeer a Humvee. He was Superman, wasn't he? In fact, she didn't speak much at all as he strapped her in. She couldn't take her eyes off him while he stood a few feet away, deep in conversation with Eritrea.

Eritrea nodded a few times, shook her head a few times. Once, she held her left hand up, showing Daddy her wedding ring. He took out his ticket book and wrote something on the back of a page, ripped it off, and pressed the paper into Eritrea's hand. She walked back with him to the Humvee.

"Okay, Reesie." Eritrea smiled. "It's been real. I'm gonna wait around here for Dré to show up."

She reached out to squeeze Reesie's clenched hands

and leaned closer. "Take it from a sister: don't hold this stuff in for too long. You got nothing to beat yourself up about. Promise you'll find somebody to let it all out with, okay?"

Find somebody? Who? Find someplace. Where? Home wasn't even home anymore. Reesie didn't answer.

Daddy got in and started the engine. Reesie looked back and saw Eritrea's skinny figure getting farther and farther away. She was still waving with both hands. Reesie felt odd and lonely—she'd just met Tree, but she missed her already.

Daddy began talking like they were already in the middle of a conversation. Reesie knew he was doing it to cover her unusual silence.

"So, your mama and some of the other nurses left the hospital with the first set of patients they evacuated. She's at a motel in Lafayette. Last I heard from her, you were at Miss Simon's. I've been trying to get back to the Ninth Ward, but I keep getting sent all over. It's chaos everywhere! I'm downtown, where we're supposed to be securing the Quarter, and I get word this morning that André Knight is telling every uniform he sees that he's looking for *me*. I figure his only connection is Orlando, and from Orlando to *you*, so I follow up. The trail leads me here."

He glanced at her. "That Eritrea—says she's his wife now?"

Reesie nodded.

"And she tells me y'all have been through it. But you're good. Are you?"

"I don't know. . . . Yes, I guess so. Yes." Reesie knew her police officer daddy might not be satisfied with the way she answered, but it was all she could give.

"Well." He only paused a minute before continuing his one-sided conversation.

"Listen. New Orleans is in bad shape. Between the wind damage and the flooding, it's the worst I've ever seen. I have to admit, your mama was right after all. We weren't ready. Half the force is AWOL. Communications are out. It's a zoo here, yeah! I'm gonna drop you off by your mama and head back. We gotta contain this madness till we get some help from the Feds."

"You're not coming?"

Her father glanced at her. "Can't," he said.

Reesie didn't understand. Why wasn't he joining them so they could be together? Was it her college fund again?

"Okay," Reesie said, too tired to argue. She pretended to sleep, but her brain kept replaying jumbled pictures of floating trees and dark water, angles of sunlight across a scraggly beard and ugly face. She didn't want sounds, but they came as well, until the voices from her father's radio blocked them out. There were police calls for rescues, fires, looting. One young-sounding cop with a shaky voice said he found a dead body inside a submerged car. Daddy flicked the radio off.

"What about Parraine and Tee Charmaine?" Reesie hoped her own voice would overpower the one she'd just heard.

"He got turned around and went back home. They got spotty phone service over there. All of New Orleans is without power, phones. . . . It's a bona fide disaster."

"I hope Miss Martine is all right."

"Miss Simon? What happened?"

"I'm not sure. We made it to her roof, and some people took us to the bridge, and . . . and she got sick. The medics from the National Guard took her away."

They pulled off the highway, and Reesie saw that the shoulder was lined on both sides with stopped and stalled vehicles. Eighteen-wheelers were parked between SUVs. Although some seemed abandoned, people were sitting in and outside of others, apparently camping out because they had nowhere else to go.

"Here we are," Daddy said. He pulled up behind two marked police cars.

Reesie saw her mother right away, pacing in the circular driveway in front of the motel entrance. Her shoulders were hunched and her hands were shoved deep into the pockets of the same pink uniform she must have worn when she left the house a lifetime ago.

"Oh my God! Reesie!" She ran up to the Humvee, beating on the hood as Daddy shifted into park. "Come here! Oh!" She touched Reesie's cheeks and proceeded to unbuckle the seat belt herself.

"Let her breathe, Jeannie! Let her breathe!" Daddy said.

"Are you all right?"

Reesie was unexpectedly overwhelmed, and tears rushed out again before she could find her words. Her mother stepped back with one hand over her mouth.

"What? What is it?" Mama asked. "Lloyd?" Her mother looked up at Daddy.

He tipped his head to the side, the way he did when he wanted to have a side conversation, but Mama ignored him, turning to Reesie again.

"Teresa, what is it?" she demanded.

Reesie opened her mouth, but her tongue was so dry that it stuck, and she could only clear her throat.

"She went through some stuff," her father offered.

Mama's eyebrows rose, and she spun on Daddy.

"*Stuff?* My child went through *stuff*. Just what does that mean?"

She scanned Reesie from head to toe, looking for signs that might give her the answers no one was willing to share. She fingered Reesie's ripped sleeve, and her lips trembled. Reesie looked down at her right arm and saw a red bruise, just the width of a man's hand, beginning to darken on her skin.

"Lloyd . . ." Mama's voice dropped.

Reesie said quietly, "I'm really okay, Mama. I—I got mugged. That's all." Her mother looked at her suspiciously, then spun angrily.

"This is *your* fault!" her mother burst out, and Reesie jumped, shaking all over, before realizing that of course, those words weren't directed at her. They were meant for her father.

"What? Jeannie . . ."

"Look at her! She's traumatized! She should never have been in harm's way!"

"Jeannie, nobody knew—"

"*You're* supposed to know!" her mother shouted. "Oh, Lloyd, if we'd left town, this would never have happened! If you had retired from the force two years ago, you wouldn't be running to that job! If you weren't so obstinate about the house—"

"Wait, now!" Daddy was losing his cool. "You just never really understood about the house, Jeannie!"

"Like *I* don't know what it is to give up family?"

Daddy dropped his head. Even Reesie thought that was a low blow. "Oh, Jeannie . . . ," he muttered.

People had come out to stare at them. Reesie could see the veins in her father's temples pulsing; her mother was stomping her feet on the asphalt. Reesie wanted to stop them, but she didn't know how.

"Then let's go!" Mama said. "Let's go right now. I want Reesie somewhere safe."

"I want Reesie safe too! But I can't leave, Jeannie!"

Reesie's mother stopped ranting. "You can't? Or you *won't?*" Tears sprang up in her eyes.

Reesie looked at her father and saw hurt and surprise in his eyes. She wanted to yell herself, *Stop! Please! It's not either of your faults!* But she couldn't.

"Don't make me do this, Jeannie."

Mama's voice dropped to a whisper. It was a frightening whisper.

"Why can't you walk away? You've given twenty years. I don't have a hospital anymore. We don't have a house anymore. By the grace of God, we still have our daughter. Katrina has taken almost everything I have, Lloyd. I'm not staying here."

Daddy's shoulders slumped, and for the first time ever Reesie heard his voice shake.

"Jeannie, please."

"You're making this decision, not me," Mama said, but her tone wasn't as angry as it had been. She sounded disappointed. Sad.

"Reesie and I will be on the first flight I can get to New Jersey. I'll let Junior know." Mama turned away quickly, walking toward the motel.

Reesie reluctantly took two steps to follow, then ran back to hug her father. He held her tight. So tight.

PART THREE

Staying Strong

Chapter Sixteen

DECEMBER 20, 2005

"Miss Boone. I would love to add another new piece of technology to my collection," the sarcastic voice said from the front of the classroom. "Bring it."

Reesie was more angry than embarrassed as she took her time getting up from her desk. She'd only been shutting her new cell phone off. And it was clear that this Mr. Worthy had it in for her anyway. Every time she'd opened her mouth in his class, he had that smirk on his face like she couldn't speak English or something.

One of the other kids had told her that it wasn't her New Orleans accent, really—that he was just mean—but she didn't believe it. She eased out from her chair, and low-level whispers and a few snickers followed her to the front of the room.

Nothing had gone quite right in the three months since she'd come to Montclair, New Jersey. Sure, this middle school was pretty cool, and it was actually fun living with her aunt, uncle, and little cousins. Jazz, the six-year-old, even called Reesie her "big sister." But her father was still in New Orleans, her mother was still barely speaking to him, Junior was in college, and their home had drowned along with everything they owned.

Sometimes, like now, she wanted to scream to the world, *Do you know what I'm dealing with?* But that seemed so unlike her real Reesie self. Sometimes, like now, she didn't even know if that Reesie existed anymore. So she went through the motions.

Worthy gave her his famous withering stare when she made eye contact with him at his desk. Annoyed, she dropped her phone with a clatter, just out of reach of his open hand. She knew he would take points off her already low algebra grade, but it was hard to care.

"Well, we don't tolerate that attitude here, Miss Boone. See me for detention this afternoon."

Reesie kept cool as she walked back to her seat and slouched in it, but her conscience was screaming and hollering. Another detention! Her mother would lose it. And who was supposed to pick up Jazz from school now?

Reesie violently flipped open her notebook, telling her righteous self that she might get away with it, since Mama and Daddy weren't exactly standing together on very much these days. She sighed and began to copy the freakishly long equation from the chalkboard, frowning with forced concentration. The bell rang before she could get everything down. On cue, Mr. Worthy turned and wiped the dry-erase board clean. *Just for spite*, she thought, scrambling to gather her things so she could make it to Art I on time.

The art class was a welcoming world for her. It was the one place where she most remembered her old life—the best parts. They were drawing still lifes for this unit, and when her pencil touched paper, she was in the moment. Lemons in a silver bowl, a blue glass vase beside it, a red cloth draped behind. There was nothing before or after, only what her eyes saw and what her brain created in the moment.

The period was over before she knew it.

Heat was blasting in the hallway, which seemed to have shrunk as it filled with preteen bodies, voices, and smells. She got a momentary dizzy, stomach-tightening feeling that took her back to the Superdome on that awful day. This was almost too much for her to handle. She quickly squeezed through to the staircase, hurrying to her locker. It was practically empty. She stood for a moment, mentally ticking off the textbooks she was using as a side table in her room: history, earth science . . . and yes, algebra. At least she could make an attempt at the homework.

Was she going to the detention? *Not*.

She heard two or three hi's from girls she passed, and got four or five what's-up nods from boys as she hustled her way toward the side doors. There was no sign of Felicidad, Dadi, the only girl she'd met on her first day who'd actually *not* asked her a question about New Orleans. Reesie was willing to be friends with her for that reason alone. She remembered that Dadi, a fierce dancer, had a tap class after school on Tuesdays.

Maybe she should call Ayanna, or Orlando. . . . One touch of her jacket pocket reminded her that one, she didn't have a phone, and two, they were hundreds of miles away. Orlando was still in Houston, but they were closer friends than ever, even if they hadn't ever talked about that kiss. Ayanna, on the other hand, was getting slower and slower on picking up now that her family had decided to stay in Atlanta.

Reesie sucked her teeth in disgust.

She pushed out of the heavy steel doors, and her foot sank into snow. She hated snow. She lifted her face to the gray-blue sky, feeling the big wet flakes on her eyelashes and lips, almost like rain.

Almost like water, she thought, as she slogged her lime green, fleece-lined boots through it. In one movement, she tugged at the straps of the stiff purple backpack that she despised, and hunched her shoulders to wade through the soft ankle-deep snow. Almost like water.

And then, predictable as always, everything came back to her. Those memories that hid in the shadows when she tried to sleep. Those vivid thoughts that hung like bats in the back of her mind during algebra. Those memories that kept her distant from nearly all these supposedly *good* kids in this *good* school in this *good* New Jersey town.

She stomped along the unshoveled sidewalks. The trees arching over her hung heavy with icicles from a freeze and then a thaw a few days before. The different-colored houses she passed all wore holiday decorations, wreaths and lights strung across Victorian porches. Some even had stupid-looking inflated snowmen or reindeer in the middle of their front yards.

It was supposed to be the happiest time of the year, right?

Her fingers were turning numb inside the black-and-white-striped stretchy gloves she wore. She couldn't get used to the cold. Everything up here was so different! She looked up to see the redbrick elementary school building looming against that dingy sky. Across the park next to it, two half-grown kids were wallowing in the snow, whooping and laughing.

Rainbow colors were all she could make out through the fogged-up windows of the Hillside school cafeteria, where the little kids waited to be picked up. The door flew open and Jazz flew out.

"Snow again!" She was as thrilled as those kids in the park. Reesie smiled but didn't show any teeth. Hers were chattering anyway.

"Yeah," she answered. "So, what trouble did you get into today?"

Jazz grabbed her hand, and Reesie felt a funny little flutter inside. It was nice to be around little kids.

"No trouble. I made up a new song!"

Jazz was dancing in the snow, using her footprints to make swirls and loops. She was always dancing . . . or singing.

"Booonie! Booonie Girls! Aunty Jean and you make two! Boo—"

Reesie loved being a "big sister," but she wasn't feeling Jazz's little song. They really *weren't* the Boone family anymore, with Daddy still in New Orleans four months after he promised they would be together.

Jazz stopped, swung her braids, and put her hands on her hips.

"You're mad. You're not my make-believe sister anymore?"

Everything she'd let build up inside shook Reesie at once: fury, confusion, and shame. She looked away from Jazz so she wouldn't explode.

"Yes," she finally said. "Yes, I'm your make-believe sister."

"Still?" Jazz managed to skip ahead a few paces.

"Still," Reesie said, pulling her house key out. "But you know, I'll be going back home one day."

"To New Orleans?" They shook their boots off on the steps of the wide yellow house.

"Yes. To New Orleans."

Jazz shook her head, and the tassels on her striped elf hat swung around her head. "Noooo . . . ," she said slowly. "There's no more New Orleans!"

Reesie wasn't about to argue with a six-year-old, and she wondered if maybe Jazz was right. What if home wasn't really home anymore?

She blinked at the wreath her mother and aunt had

made of huge scarlet poinsettias and hung on the dark-wood-and-stained-glass front doors. Snow had blown across the porch, almost covering something lying near the tiny potted Christmas tree by the mailbox. Jazz bent to pick it up.

"Ree-see Boo-ne," she read out loud proudly. "You got a package!" She shoved the brown-paper-wrapped rectangle at Reesie, then stood on her toes to get the rest of the mail from the box.

Reesie unlocked the front door and almost tripped over the stuffed animal zoo scattered in the front hall. She peeled off her layers, dropped them at the foot of the stairs, and glanced at the return address on the box. Her heart sped up. It was from Daddy!

She ripped and tossed paper on her way to the living room, glad that Jazz had made a beeline for cookies and milk.

A leather, emerald green sketchbook was tucked between sheets of green tissue paper. Reesie slowly thumbed through the pages. They were all blank, big enough for design sketches on one side with space for fabric swatches and notes on the other. She closed the book gently.

Though she loved her art class, no one in it knew she wanted to become a fashion designer. And she

134

couldn't remember the last time she'd sewn anything or drawn even a stick figure wearing clothes. How did he know?

A smaller box of colored pencils had fallen onto the cushion beside her . . . and there was a note.

Reesie—Thought I'd get a head start on the Christmas shopping. Hope you can use this. Show me some outrageous design when I see you on Christmas Eve!

Love, Daddy

Reesie crumpled the tissue paper in her excitement. He was coming!

Keys jangled in the kitchen door. Reesie had forgotten that her mother was working an early shift this week. The door opened and slammed. There was more banging, of groceries heaped onto the counter, then keys smacked onto the table. Reesie rushed in the direction of the sounds.

Her glowing, grinning face met her mother's scowling, vexed one. Jazz hopped off her chair and danced around the two of them, humming her new Boonie Girls tune.

"Guess what?" Mama sucked her teeth as if *she* were the middle-school student.

"Daddy's coming for Christmas!" mother and daughter both said at once. Then, in stunned silence, they each took in the other's reaction.

"Ho, ho ho!" Jazz sang out loud, but changed her lyrics. "Boonie Girls glad and mad!"

Chapter Seventeen

Reesie's Christmas spirit continued to rise. The next day, her mother agreed to allow her to go shopping with Dadi at the mall. Then Aunt Tish, who had won quite a few awards for her television acting, had intervened at school to get Reesie's phone back. More important than any of that—most important—was the text Orlando had sent while her phone was locked away in Worthy's room.

B N NJ @ XMAS!

That afternoon, Reesie showed Dadi the message before she bit into a Jamaican patty in the food court. It was the closest thing she'd discovered to a Louisiana meat pie.

Dadi sat across from her, peppering her with questions. With her mouth and hands full, Reesie couldn't answer her friend right away.

"I bet you can't wait! What are you going to do? When's he getting here? Where's the first place you're going to take him? When can I meet your boyfriend?" Dadi stared at Reesie with her eyes twinkling, propping her skinny olive elbows onto the table. "You *must* miss him like crazy."

"Felicidad, I told you that Orlando is not my boyfriend!" Reesie washed down the last of the flaky crust with orange soda.

"But it's *amazing* that your boyfriend is coming all the way up here to *see* you!" Dadi hadn't touched her cheese fries yet, but Reesie knew she'd scarf that order down and then get another, because according to her, a dancer's metabolism made her hungry all the time.

"He's not my boyfriend."

"Well, he kissed you."

"In the middle of a hurricane when he was out of his mind looking for his brother! It was a freak-out kiss."

Since Orlando had never mentioned it, Reesie found it hard to convince herself now that he'd meant anything by the kiss, although he hadn't failed to text every day since he'd found her, and even called when Dré and Tree had hitchhiked their way to Texas. . . .

"Reesie, are you listening to me? You never listen to

138

anybody. Maybe that's why you haven't made more friends at school." Dadi was inhaling her last two fries. "I don't mean to hurt your feelings, but sometimes you're out there . . . like, not *here*, where the real world is."

Dadi's comment irritated Reesie a little, and that tiny spark of anger made her want to talk.

"It was my birthday that day, you know? Birthdays won't ever be the same for me."

"Wow." Dadi stopped chewing. "You mean the Katrina day? You never said!"

"Yeah. Maybe the problem at school is y'all don't understand what the real world is!"

Dadi pouted and crossed her arms. "I'm included in that? I thought we were friends. You never told me *anything*, except about your boyfriend."

Reesie squirmed uncomfortably in her seat. She was grateful that a loud family with rustling shopping bags hustled into the booth next to them.

"I was with my neighbor. She's, like, eighty. She was making—made—my birthday cake. And Orlando's brother showed up—"

"Wait! The one he was looking for when he kissed you?" Her voice got louder, and a girl near their table snickered. Reesie made a face, but now that she'd started talking, she didn't want to stop.

"Yeah. We got through the hurricane okay, but the flood started after. The water inside the house was almost as high as the ceiling. We went up into the attic, and then chopped a hole in the roof to get out."

Dadi's eyes were wide.

"We sat up there all night, till some fishing guys rescued us in their boat."

"On a *roof*! Was it scary?"

"Yeah."

"Then everything was okay?"

"Not even. Some soldiers took us to the Superdome." Reesie blew out a long breath. Nope, she wasn't going that far. "I can't even—anyway, Miss Martine—my neighbor? Something happened and she got sick. These soldier guys just took her away."

"But where? What happened then?"

"I don't know. We still haven't been able to find her. My dad found me—" Reesie decided to leave another part of the story out. "And we didn't have a home to go back to, so my mom and I came here. Dad's a police officer, so . . ." Reesie shrugged.

Dadi shook her head. "I saw that stuff on TV, but I never thought . . ."

"Nobody thinks much about New Orleans except folks from New Orleans," Reesie said, pushing her chair made everything look beautiful. It was like a scene from a movie. Orlando would get a kick out of falling snow.

Reesie shook her head and sighed, trudging back up the driveway. It was time for a serious conversation with her mother.

"Mom? We need to talk." Reesie's voice sounded formal and stiff, even to her own ears, when she entered the kitchen. Somehow in the last few weeks she had stopped calling her mother *Mama*, the New Orleans way. Now she said *Mom*.

"Jeannie, let me handle the stove," Aunt Tish said, looking at Reesie curiously.

"Don't let it burn!" Reesie's mother said, handing her sister the spoon. Aunt Tish bowed dramatically and made a face, but Reesie didn't smile the way she usually would. She stepped into the dining room, where her mother was standing, her arms folded.

"Mom, I'm sorry."

"For the detention, or for being rude in the car?" Mom raised her eyebrows.

"Both, I guess." Reesie took a deep breath. "When you said I should move on . . . I—I can't!"

"Reesie—" Mom's face softened, and she dropped her arms. Reesie took a step back in case her mother was about to hug her. She couldn't take that, not yet.

back. "I don't want to talk about this anymore. I need to find my daddy a Christmas present!"

Dadi grabbed her purse. With a wide grin, she flipped the mood.

"Okay. Got any great ideas? How about a G.I. Joe?"

"What? You are so silly!" Reesie was glad to smile at Dadi's little joke. She'd done well in her choice of a new friend.

"Oh! Oh!" Reesie pulled Dadi into a music store. "I know what to get both of my parents!"

"What?"

Reesie made for the old-school funk aisle and rifled through the CDs.

"Listen. You have to hear a sample. Is this song perfect, or what?" She shoved headphones onto her friend and watched Dadi's face as she pulled one of the earbuds to her own head.

"It's Parliament, from the seventies," Reesie said, singing along. " 'I just want to testify . . . what your love has done for meeee!' They love this. I'm gonna get them both the same CD!"

"Your cousin is rubbing off on you!" Dadi said.

The girls laughed. They were still humming and giggling when they rushed outside a little later to catch their ride with Reesie's mom.

"Well," her mother said, eyeing Reesie in the rearview mirror, "I'm glad you can find something to laugh about!"

Reesie rustled her shopping bags and tried hard not to roll her eyes. That might only pull a detention in Worthy's world, but in Jeannie's world? Trouble with a capital *T.*

"What do you mean?" Reesie asked calmly.

"Mr. Worthy called for a conference. You skipped a *detention* yesterday?"

Dadi dropped her head and started humming something more like a death march. Reesie pursed her lips together, knowing that her mother wouldn't say any more until she'd dropped Dadi off. The car was filled with icy silence all the way back to town. Dadi mouthed the words *good luck* when she got out at her house.

"Now, Teresa . . ."

"Mom, I—"

"This school rebellion thing has gone far enough. No colleges or fashion schools are going to take a first look at Ds."

"Mom, that's years away! And—and it's just hard, okay?"

Her mother screeched to a halt in Aunt Tish's driveway and turned around in the car.

"I already made the conference appointment. An[d] have arranged for you to see a psychologist."

Reesie forgot herself completely, and yelled, "A wh[at?] Now I'm crazy?"

"Teresa Arielle Boone, do not speak to me in th[at] tone. You've got to deal with whatever happened an[d] then move on."

Reesie gasped in disbelief. How could her mother sa[y] such a thing? She angrily fumbled for the handle an[d] threw the door open.

"How come this is about *me?*" she continued yelling, hoping that the neighbors would hear. "You and Daddy haven't moved on, you just moved apart! If you're looking for who's crazy, I'm not the one!"

"Reesie! Teresa!" Instead of going inside, Reesie stalked off. Halfway down the block, fresh snowflakes blew against her face, and she stopped. Slowly, she turned back.

Should she pretend to be her old self, a "good girl," just to get through the holidays? Daddy was coming, and Junior and . . . Orlando.

She watched the snow, backlit by a streetlight, tumble to Earth with amazing perfection. Nobody had ever told her how blindingly bright the new clean snow could be, even at night. She had to admit that it

"I *can't* move on, 'cause I feel like I'm waiting on something! I don't know how to explain it. All this time, since Katrina, I've been waiting. Waiting to sketch and sew again. Waiting to see if this thing with Orlando is anything. . . ."

"Orlando?" Mom pulled out a chair and sat down.

Reesie shook her head. It wasn't Orlando that she wanted to talk about right now.

"Waiting for you and Daddy to be in one house again!"

"Well, Reesie that's—that's complicated," Mom said quietly.

"No, I know it's my fault!" Reesie blurted out. Her voice shook. "I heard you and Daddy arguing. He could have stopped working, but because of me, he stayed! And—and now you're going to break up, and—"

"Reesie! That wasn't really about you, and that is *not* your fault. We're not—"

"It is! And it's my fault that everything is screwed up with fixing our house, because I had all the insurance papers and stuff in my backpack, and I let that man take it! And—" Reesie was crying, her mother was crying.

"Stop." Mom came closer. "Stop, now. I wish you'd told me this before, honey. None of this, none of it, is on you."

"I just want to go back to New Orleans, to my real

life again!" Reesie mumbled into her mother's shoulder. "Is that so wrong?"

"No, baby. It's not wrong." Mom rubbed Reesie's back the way she used to when Reesie had a stomachache or a falling out with Ayanna. Reesie was surprised that it still made her feel calmer.

"Why don't we both try really hard to make this a *right* Christmas, not just a white one, huh?"

"Okay." Reesie sniffed and wiped her wet face. The dining room's swinging door creaked, and Reesie managed to giggle through her tears. Aunt Tish had been listening in on everything.

Chapter Eighteen

December 23, 2005

Reesie was actually tingling all over, and it wasn't from the fitted wool turtleneck she wore layered under a denim jumper and her brother's old hoodie. Finally the last day of classes before the holidays had come. Aunt Tish had picked her up from school. Now they were zooming on the Garden State Parkway toward Newark, toward the train station. In just about forty-five minutes, she would see Daddy.

"So, are you going to just burst?" Aunt Tish glanced over at her as she turned down the radio Christmas carols.

Reesie laughed a little, because she could barely sit still.

"Maybe." She stared through the windshield of the

BMW, unable to tell her aunt how anxious she was about her father's visit. She blinked at the blur of cars and green parkway signs as they sped along, and her mind raced with them.

Would Daddy be disappointed that her grades hadn't really improved? And what would he say when he found out that her new sketchbook had just one lonely drawing in it? The design wasn't very good, either. Reesie wondered about bigger things too. Was he coming to take them home?

She wiggled in the warm seat.

At least she and her mom were getting along. They understood each other better since that night in the dining room, and Reesie knew she didn't have to pretend anymore that she wasn't hurting and confused inside. Maybe she *could* learn to move on. She sighed and smiled at a Christmas tree outside a gas station decorated with hubcaps and blinking colored lights.

"Well, I tell you . . . ," Aunt Tish was saying. "Your mood sure has changed since the other day. You finally sleeping all night, huh?"

"Yes, and I had a regular dream too—not a nightmare. It was about Miss Simon's book." Her voice trailed off.

"What book?"

"Well, Miss Martine used to be this big writer. She

had a book published a long, long time ago, called *Woman Everlasting*. I—I lost it in the flood."

"Oh. I didn't know she was a writer." Aunt Tish glanced over at her. "Was she any good?"

"I didn't get a chance to read it," Reesie said.

"That's a shame! Maybe you can find a copy at the Strand bookstore in New York. I'll take you over there."

"Great! Thanks."

Aunt Tish paused for a few minutes, and Reesie knew there was going to be a shift in conversation. Aunt Tish was never shy about digging into somebody's business.

"I'm really glad you had a heart-to-heart with your mother. She's worried about you. This whole thing has been hard on her."

Reesie looked sideways at her aunt. All this time she'd been focused on what *Reesie* went through in New Orleans. She had never even thought about what her mother must have gone through, not knowing if her daughter and husband were even alive. It must have been terrible for her. And then there was the crazy, no-turning-back fight with Daddy, on top of losing her job and her house. She was a thousand miles away from her son, too, and Reesie's recent attitude issues here at the Montclair middle school probably hadn't made things any easier.

Her mother was not only Mom; she was Jeannie Boone, a flesh-and-blood woman. Reesie had never thought about that before. Her mother was also doing her best to deal with an experience that had completely turned her life upside down. Mom deserved better, especially from her only daughter. Maybe the best present Reesie could give her mother this Christmas would be to try a little bit harder—at just about everything.

Aunt Tish pulled the Beamer into the parking lot, and Reesie shivered as she stepped outside. They hurried across the street and into Newark's Penn Station.

"Oh, look!" Aunt Tish pointed up at the huge display of train arrivals, clicking and rolling up new times and tracks. There it was: CRESCENT FROM NEW ORLEANS, ARRIVING, TRACK 5.

Reesie ran, weaving between holiday travelers loaded down with suitcases and crying babies. She flung open the glass door and bounded up the stairs, leaving Aunt Tish behind. The train threw off heat on the chilly platform and belched out steam as it glided to a complete stop.

Reesie rocked from one foot to the other, watching nervously as the doors slid open. Grandmothers and college students streamed out. Cranky kids stumbled forth with lumpy pillows under their arms. A tiny dark-haired woman squealed and rushed to hug a soldier and his huge duffel, both in camouflage.

"Well, Miss Reesie Bear Boone! Look at *you!*"

Reesie spun toward that raspy voice. There he was!

"Daddy!" Her father's strong arms were around her at once, and he swung her completely up off the ground, just like he had when he'd found her at the Superdome.

"I can't believe it's you, for real!" Reesie squeezed her father's arm, breathing in his familiar musk aftershave.

"Oh, so Dad gets all the props, and the brother who showed you how to ride a bike is just iced out?"

Junior was loping toward them, all arms and legs like their father, with the same round walnut-brown face as their mother. He was loaded down with a computer bag, backpack, and too many shopping bags.

"Junior! I thought you were taking the bus!" Reesie reached out, without letting her father go, to grab Junior's collar. She couldn't believe she was actually hugging both of them, live and in person.

"Oh, look, Dad! Little Bear is gonna cry!" Junior said in his most annoying older-brother teasing voice.

"Oh, shut up!" Reesie punched him in the shoulder.

"Business as usual." Daddy shook his head, watching them. Reesie saw the pride in his eyes. She cut hers at Junior.

"Just 'cause you're in *college* . . . ," she muttered, taking his computer bag and one of the shopping bags. It was amazingly heavy. She glanced down.

"Don't you dare look, nosy!" Junior adjusted to his lighter load.

"Hey, Daddy," Reesie said, "if you carried all this on, how much stuff did you *check*?"

"You're dipping into Santa Claus's eggnog now, Reesie. What's your mama doing, anyway? Parking in New York?"

Reesie fell off her cloud nine with a thump. He expected Mom to meet him at the station? Although her mother had reassured Reesie that things were better between them, this looked bad, very bad. She glanced at Junior, who mouthed, *Where is she?*

"Lloyd Boone!" Aunt Tish sang out his name dramatically, so that even strangers stopped to look. "How in the world are you, brother-in-law?" She swept past Reesie and took her father's arm. "Jeannie is so caught up in making things just right for you that I volunteered to trek down here. Baggage pickup is this way. How are things coming along in the Big Easy?"

"Still trying to keep the peace and still digging ourselves out of Mississippi River mud," Daddy said. Aunt Tish followed immediately with another question, and for the moment New Orleans was their only topic.

"Is Mom avoiding him on purpose?" Junior whispered.

Reesie tried to sound positive. "I really thought she was finishing up a double shift. Maybe she and Aunt Tish are cooking something up!"

"I hope it's red beans and rice. Dining hall food is the worst, and Dad is not too swift at the stove."

Reesie elbowed him, slowing down as she watched her father and Aunt Tish round a corner underneath a BAGGAGE CLAIM sign.

"What's it like at his apartment?" she asked. There had been so much damage at their house that her father couldn't live in it.

"Well, it's real small, and—"

"Wait. Never mind that. You can tell me later. What does it feel like being at the house now? You said you've been going on weekends to help clean up, so . . ."

Junior shook his head slowly. "Honestly?"

"Honestly."

"There's nothing left, Reesie."

He had to be kidding, making some kind of sick

brother joke. "You mean stuff got wrecked," Reesie said. "I saw what the wind did—"

"*Water* is the most dangerous element in the universe, girl. It took a week for all the floodwater to go down, and it took a while after that for Dad to get back to the house. He said the watermark was at the ceiling. Everything made from wood was soft. Soft! The carpets were already mildewy, and mold was growing on the kitchen walls."

Reesie gasped and wrinkled her nose. "That's like poison," she said.

"Yeah. We had to wear heavy-duty masks and some kind of hazmat suits to get rid of all our furniture and appliances and clothes."

"Clothes?" She'd thought—hoped—that some things might have been saved.

He looked sincerely sympathetic. "Dad pulled down a section of Sheetrock last week when I came down, and there was crazy mold inside the walls, too."

A faint "oh" was Reesie's only response.

"I don't see how we can ever go back. Dad's in denial about it, but we'd have to tear that thing down and build it back again!"

"Don't call our house 'that thing'!" she said. "I mean, I know it sounds bad."

"Yeah. It's bad."

"You two coming, or you gonna stand there all day catching up?"

Daddy and Aunt Tish were halfway to the exit. Reesie shifted the heavy bag to her other hand. This holiday was going to be much tougher than she'd imagined.

Chapter Nineteen

During the ride to the house, they stayed away from New Orleans talk, with the attention mostly on Junior's college life: Daddy bragged on his record-breaking back-stroke, Aunt Tish asked about girlfriends. Junior tried, very obviously, Reesie thought, to avoid the word *grades*. She would normally have been cracking up over making him squirm, but her mind was on other things. What would happen when her parents were finally in the same room?

They slammed out of the car, and Aunt Tish popped the trunk before she crunched across the snow to open the kitchen door. The spicy aroma of red beans and sausage wafted out on the warm air. Reesie relaxed, even as she dragged Junior's heavy duffel bag. Mom was home, all right, and she'd been cooking Daddy's favorites. That was a good sign.

While Junior muttered about his load, Reesie followed her father inside without taking her eyes off him. He strode past the pots steaming on the stove, moving straight through the open dining room door. Reesie stopped short.

Her father had spotted her mother in the next room. Aunt Tish, who'd been standing beside her sister, instantly vanished.

"Missed you at the station," Daddy said, easing his arms around their mother's waist and nuzzling his chin into her neck. He whispered something else to her.

"Lloyd." She didn't say it with a laugh, or even with much love, but her body seemed to go limp against him. Then she turned around and kissed him.

Junior crashed into Reesie's back. They were both momentarily paralyzed by what they were watching.

"Yes!" Reesie pumped her fist and turned to high-five her brother. Junior didn't look so cheerful.

Reesie's smile faded, and she let the swinging door close. "What's the matter with you?" she asked.

Junior shrugged. "I'm just saying . . ." He opened the fridge and stood there, eyeball-shopping like he was in the grocery store freezer aisle.

"What? And get out of Aunt Tish's refrigerator!"

"I'm not so sure Mom and Dad are going to just make up and play nice. Dad probably won't admit this, but he feels like Mom abandoned him, and I kinda think he's right."

"*What?*" Reesie wanted to call him wrong, but she couldn't get the words out.

"Life is not a movie," Junior said, his back to her. "In real life, stuff hits the fan, a man wants his lady to be there for him, and she ups and leaves. Now, in the movie version, some slow music would play and they'd meet up by accident and hook up again like nobody was hurting. Girl, everybody in New Orleans was hurting! I think Mom should've hung in."

"Are you *serious?*" she said angrily. "You weren't even there, you don't know—" She caught herself before she added, "They were fighting over me!" *Not the time*, she told herself. *Not the time.*

"Listen, don't jump all over me. You want me to say that I predict Dad and Mom will be like newlyweds by the time that ball drops on New Year's Eve? Okay. Your fantasy." He turned to see his sister's unhappy expression, and he softened his tone. "I don't mean that they've stopped loving, but there is some deep anger they gotta work out."

Reesie said nothing. Was Junior right? Had her mother abandoned her father? Was the thing between them *not* about her, or his job, at all? She slipped back to inch open the dining room door, not knowing what to expect.

Their parents were sitting together on the sofa, their heads together as they spoke in low voices. That didn't look like deep anger. They were talking, and it had to mean something. She didn't care what Junior's two cents were.

Before Reesie could ease away, Daddy looked directly up at her.

"Come on in, Reesie. We won't bite you—or each other," he said, waving her in with one arm and keeping the other around Mom's shoulders.

Reesie's heart began to beat fast. Then her mother patted a spot on the sofa and smiled, looking younger somehow.

"Really, it's okay," she said. They seemed so much the way they used to be, so close to their hugging, kissing displays of affection that embarrassed Reesie and Junior and entertained their friends. So close.

Reesie walked slowly past the brass reindeer marching through tinsel across Aunt Tish's dining room mantel. She blinked as the sparkling ball decorations on the

Christmas tree shook and shimmered, bouncing points of light into the huge mirror between the front windows. Everything was reflected there: her parents' bodies so close that they formed one shape; Reesie's own expression of anxious hope. She looked away.

"We want to talk," her mother said. Reesie sat down beside her.

"Hey, Lloyd Edward Boone Jr.!" Daddy called loudly.

Junior appeared holding a double-decker sandwich with both hands.

"Mmmm?" He'd taken a bite out of it.

"Get in here. Your mother and I have something to say!"

Junior sauntered in, draped himself over an upholstered armchair, and then took one look at his father and slid to the floor.

"Sorry," he mumbled. "S'up?"

Reesie wanted to throw something at him. After the conversation they'd just had in the kitchen, he couldn't imagine what was up?

"A couple of things," Daddy said. He leaned forward. That was when Reesie noticed one of the bags he'd carried off the train, sitting between his feet. He reached into it and pulled out a pale blue envelope.

"Reesie first. This is for you."

She took the envelope and turned it over, squinting at the spidery old-fashioned script that read, *Miss Teresa Boone*.

"You found her! You found Miss Martine!" Reesie shouted, ripping the letter open.

"Oh, read it to us!" Mama said, sounding as excited as Reesie felt.

"Okay." The single sheet of paper trembled in Reesie's hands.

Dear Teresa,

I hope this letter finds you safe with your family. Lloyd and Jeannie have done excellent work in raising a girl like you. I want to thank you for showing an old woman how to put up a stiff fight. Eritrea has told me that you stayed strong. I hope you grow up to find everything in life you are looking for.

Sincerely,

Martine Odette Simon

"Wow," Junior said. "She's talking about *you*?"

"You chill out, brother!" Daddy shot at him. Reesie

paid Junior no attention for once. She reread the note in silence.

"I really had to do my policeman thing to locate her," Daddy said. "She had heart surgery and she's staying in a rehab place in Baton Rouge."

"Thanks, Daddy." Reesie smiled at her father.

"That André is a pretty surprising young man, seeing after her the way he did," Daddy said. He dug into the bag again, this time pulling out a small box, which he placed on his wife's lap.

"Lloyd! We weren't going to exchange gifts—"

He quieted her with another kiss, and Junior made a face. Reesie smiled, and when her mother gave her a should-I-open-it? look, Reesie nodded eagerly.

Her mother opened the box. At first Reesie couldn't see what it was that her mother grasped to her heart. She covered her face with her other hand and started to cry softly. Reesie leaned against her shoulder, and even Junior stopped chewing.

"What is it?" He crawled forward on his knees to see.

"It's—it's . . ." Mama couldn't quite compose herself. Reesie peeled her fingers back to reveal a small, very plain gold heart, no bigger than a nickel. She'd never seen it before.

Daddy cleared his throat. "This is the first piece of jewelry—"

"First gift," Mama corrected him gently.

"The first gift I ever gave your mom. I was working and still in school. Saved up three months to buy it at Maison Blanche so she'd have a fancy name on the box. I found it, crazy enough, wedged in a baseboard in our bedroom after I emptied it out."

Reesie stared at her brother. What was it he'd said, about there still being love between them? Ma Maw would have said that the gold heart, stuck in the room they'd shared for twenty years, was a sign.

"Jeannie." Daddy's voice changed, at once reminding Reesie of that day outside the Lafayette motel. "Jeannie, you know Pete and I watched our mother work two and three jobs to buy that house so she could move us out of the projects. That house is her legacy!"

"I know, Lloyd. I know how much more than a house it is to you."

"But it's not family." His voice was thick. "Jeannie, I'm asking . . . I'm begging you. Please come back. Nothing is home without you and Reesie."

Reesie gulped down the lump in her throat. Her mother fingered the gold heart, but she didn't answer right away. What did that mean? Surely, Mom wasn't thinking of saying no, was she?

"You—we—worked so hard for everything, and now it's all just *gone*!" her mother said. Daddy hung his head, and Reesie could see that he was trying to maintain control.

"But, Mom!" she interrupted. "Everything *isn't* gone! *We're* here—together—for Christmas. This is what I've been waiting for. We *want* to be together! That makes us kind of a home without a house, doesn't it?"

"The kid is making sense, Mom," Junior added. "Say yes. Just—please, say yes!"

Mom methodically began to take off the necklace she was wearing, and carefully slid the old heart onto the chain. When she lifted her arms to return the chain to her neck, Daddy fastened it.

"You Boones are ganging up on me!" she finally said with a sigh. She looked at Daddy. "I'll try, Lloyd. Reesie and I will come for spring break. Then we'll figure it out."

Reesie and Junior cheered loudly.

"Merry Christmas to me!" Daddy said, kissing her again.

Reesie knew that one week of vacation wasn't forever, but she didn't care. She was happier than she'd dared to be in months. And a short time later they were in Aunt Tish's kitchen just like always: together, laughing, home.

Chapter Twenty

"Reesie! You're going to wear a hole in that rug if you don't stop pacing like that!" Aunt Tish came and stood close to Reesie at the window.

"He said they'd be here at two," she said. She didn't take her eyes away from the window, because then she might miss Uncle Jimmy's black Escalade as it pulled up to the curb.

"Honey, they're driving through ice and snow to get here."

Reesie smiled in spite of her nervousness.

"You know, I went on a date with Jimmy once," Aunt Tish said, clasping her hands behind her back to peer out the window too.

"Are you *serious*?" Reesie laughed.

"Well, it was years before I met your uncle Teddy. I was visiting New Orleans during spring break. He's a nice guy. Just wasn't *the* guy. Know what I mean?" Aunt Tish winked.

"Yeah!" Reesie would have felt weird having this kind of talk with any other adult. But somehow with Aunt Tish it seemed as natural as talking to Dadi or Ayanna— or Orlando.

"So Jimmy's nephew—"

"Orlando."

"Orlando! Nice name. He talked Jimmy into coming all the way up here to see you? I think he's a friend you should keep," she said.

Reesie turned at the odd way her aunt said the word *keep*, and saw another mischievous twinkle in her eyes.

"Oh, look! Here they are!" Aunt Tish said calmly, pulling the curtain back. Reesie stumbled around her to the front door and threw it open. A light snow was falling. Jimmy was carefully lining up his SUV with the curb. Orlando's face was turned away from the front passenger window. He'd cut his hair! The neat black waves brushed close to his head made his shoulders seem wider-than-real.

Reesie stepped out into the freezing air without feeling cold at all and yelled, "Hey! Hey! Over here!"

Orlando whipped around in his seat and his grin lit up the interior of the car—at least it seemed to. He opened the door while the Escalade was still moving. Jimmy shouted, but Orlando didn't seem to care. He unhooked his seat belt and jumped out.

Of course, his feet slid on the slick sidewalk and he lost his balance, flying face-first into a snowbank just outside the picket fence. When he looked up, he was laughing. Reesie hopped down the steps and skidded toward the fence to yank the gate open. By accident or on purpose, she tumbled too—and landed spread-eagle like a snow angel beside him.

"Where you at, Peanut Butter?" Orlando was still laughing, wet snow on his eyelashes.

"I'm right here with Frosty the Snowman!" She grinned, her lips numbing.

"Y'all get up outta that snow and come get these coolers!" Uncle Jimmy bellowed. Orlando pulled himself up and offered a hand to Reesie.

"I don't know how you stand this stuff for a whole winter." He shook his head, and wet melting drops flew off his hair. He looked up at the sky and laughed again.

"This is crazy!"

Reesie punched him in the shoulder, and he grabbed her in a bear hug. They ignored Uncle Jimmy for a minute, standing on the sidewalk. She had to force herself not to cry.

"I'm so glad to see you!" she whispered.

"Back at you, girl!" he said.

"Break it up, break it up!" Uncle Jimmy was all of two hundred and fifty pounds, and in his shearling coat and fur hat, he looked like a big bear coming around the Escalade. He grinned at Reesie the way he always did.

"Good to see you, Reesie. Now, you two get these coolers of hot sausage and crawfish into your Aunt Tish's house." He leaned toward her and lowered his loud voice. "And tell me: is this Teddy joker that she married more handsome than me for real?"

Reesie, laughing again, stepped back from him, as if she were giving the idea serious thought.

"Sorry, Jimmy." She pretended to have a sad face. "But I think Teddy's got you beat. You're a real nice guy, though!"

Uncle Jimmy grunted. "Nice guy. All my life I've been the nice guy," he joked, unlocking the back of the SUV.

"L-let's hurry up!" Orlando's breath puffed in front of his face, and Reesie giggled at how freaked he was by the cold weather.

"Okay, okay!" She pulled crumpled gloves from her jacket pocket and passed them to Orlando. Any other time, he would have gone off about the loud purple color, but now he quickly pulled them on without another word.

"I got Tony's seasoning, I got some shelled pecans, I got fresh okra and filé for the Christmas Eve gumbo," Uncle Jimmy rattled on while they lugged the coolers up onto the porch. "All I need to know is where I can get the shrimp and crabmeat, and we can get this party started!"

Reesie's mother had appeared in the doorway. "Jimmy! Welcome! What is all this?"

"Miss Jean, we brought Christmas to you from New Orleans!" He stomped the snow off his feet.

Reesie hooked Orlando's arm and scooted around her mother to pull him into the house. They came face-to-face with her father.

"Well, if it isn't Mr. Knight!" Daddy pumped Orlando's free hand. Reesie saw with amusement that Orlando's face turned even redder than it had outside.

Orlando had always talked to her about how awesome her father was, "being a cop *and* a nice dude," but whenever the two of them were in the same room, motormouth Orlando never had much to say.

"Uh—Merry Christmas, Sergeant Boone." Orlando's

eyes darted toward Reesie. Surely, he couldn't think she'd mentioned that hurricane kiss to her father? She rolled her eyes and shook her head slightly without making a sound.

"How long have I known you, boy? Call me Reesie's Dad!"

"What?" Reesie couldn't believe how ridiculous that sounded.

"Okay, Sergeant Reesie's Dad. I mean, Mr. Reesie's Dad. I mean—" Orlando sputtered nervously as her father stepped away to talk to Jimmy.

"Oh, this is too much!" Reesie said, pulling Orlando away. "Mr. Reesie's Dad?"

The hallway and living room had become a hive of grown-ups' noisy introductions and overexcited kids buzzing around, trying to get at the presents spilling out from under the Christmas tree.

"Wow! Your cousins are just as wild as my sister's kids!" Orlando shook his head, rubbing his arms with purple hands. He was shivering.

"Still cold?" Reesie asked.

"Kinda."

"Come this way." Reesie weaved through the adults and ducked into the room at the end of the hall. It was toasty warm from the blue-and-yellow flames of the gas fireplace. The only sound was some soft jazzy Christmas music coming from speakers mounted high on one wall. Orlando sank into one of the two oversize leather chairs.

"This is Aunt Tish's office," Reesie explained, closing the door.

"Sure doesn't look like any office to me," he said, craning his neck to look around.

Reesie hadn't given it much thought, but following his gaze, she agreed. The only two bookcases were filled with a mix of books and framed pictures of Aunt Tish performing onstage, or posing with other actors, some famous. On one wall, there were huge framed posters from the three movies she'd been in so far. Reesie had a déjà vu moment. This was just like Miss Martine's dining room!

"This is good," Orlando said, leaning forward. "I wanted to . . . to kinda be alone with you."

Reesie abruptly sat down in the chair facing him. Her heart was speeding in her chest, just the way it did that time she'd run her fastest fifty-yard dash. *Be alone with her?*

"I couldn't stop thinking about you!" Orlando blurted out.

Reesie felt like laughing. She felt like crying at the same time. What did he mean? Did he mean what she thought he meant? Did he mean what she wanted him to mean? But what did she want it to mean?

Instead of answering, she reached toward Orlando and peeled off one of his damp purple gloves. Her fingertips tingled with a slight electric shock.

"Ouch!" She pulled away a bit, then eased off the other glove and sat back, wadding both of them into a tight ball. He was just staring at her.

Aunt Tish suddenly breezed in with a tray holding two steaming mugs. "Thought you might like some refreshments!" she chirped.

Reesie took a deep breath, able to focus a few seconds on something other than Orlando—the smell of cinnamon and apple cider.

"You two carry on, now!" Aunt Tish said cheerfully. Then as quickly as she'd appeared, she was gone.

"I—" Reesie tried to recover her voice and her thoughts. "I guess I didn't know . . . I wasn't sure if . . . if things would be the same." She looked at him. "I mean, when we actually saw each other!" she added.

Orlando shook his head again. "Girl, things won't never be the same! We neither one of us has got a house, your family is split up; Jimmy lost his business. . . ." He threw his hands in the air, and her heart skipped a beat. Had she misunderstood?

Then he shrugged. "Everything is changed, except you and me."

Reesie smiled slowly. "Us?"

Orlando grinned. "Yeah." He picked up a mug and sipped. "What is this?"

"Cider. Apple cider." Reesie sounded impatient, but she was really working up her nerve. "So, back when you came to my house—"

He narrowed his eyes at her over the rim of the mug. "Yeah?"

She sighed. He was his old self, not making anything easy. She lowered her voice to a whisper. "When you, you know . . . *kissed* me! Was that a hurricane kiss?"

He burst into laughter, spraying cider out everywhere. "What is wrong with you? Can't a guy kiss his girl?"

"Your *girl*?"

"I convince Jimmy to drive all the way up here for Christmas, and you got some kinda confusion about how come I did it?" He faked a disgusted attitude, putting his mug down and rising from the chair. "I guess I better be gettin' to goin', then. . . ."

Reesie pulled him back. "Oh, sit down," she said.

He did. For a few minutes they only looked at each other. Reesie was calm. It was totally comfortable sitting with Orlando and not talking—she didn't think it had ever happened before. He seemed content with being quiet too. This was new.

"You're right," she finally said, thinking out loud. "Everything else did change. I can't believe it about Ayanna, can you?"

"Weird, huh?" Orlando said. "How can somebody we've been seeing every day of our lives be gone like that, no bye, no nothin'?"

"It hurts," Reesie said. She'd been having mixed feelings about how close she'd become to Felicidad while Ayanna's friendship felt more and more distant. But she knew that people had scattered from New Orleans after Katrina, *evacuees* landing all over the country. Some had definite plans to go back, like Uncle Jimmy, while others had made new lives, like Ayanna's family.

"It's unbelievable that this stuff can happen, right?" Reesie said. "I've been so scared about my parents! I still don't understand what that craziness was all about, but I think they might be making up."

"Your folks ain't divorcing, Peanut Butter."

"I just couldn't get that out of my head, that and—" She stopped. His expression didn't change; he didn't move. He was simply looking at her with the same Orlando brown eyes and the easy smile he always had for her.

Then, like the awful river breaking through the levees, her deepest fear came tumbling out of her all at once.

"I thought I was never going to see my family—you—anybody ever again." She was trembling. "I thought—I thought I was going to die," she whispered.

Orlando held her hand.

She took a deep breath. "I wish I could forget it. I have nightmares that I'm drowning. They're worse than anything that really happened."

"But you got to fight. I know you fought that dude who mugged you. Tree said you did!" Orlando said.

She nodded, with tears in her eyes, but she didn't cry. "I fought," she said.

"Bad dreams are like bad memories. So you got to keep thinking about the good stuff, to block that other stuff out." He squeezed her hand tight. "That's what I do every time it comes back to me, that scene when my mama was lying in that hospital bed, dying. I think about my sister and Dré, Jimmy starting up the restaurant again—you."

Reesie blushed.

"We fight!"

She bit her lip and nodded. "You think . . . one day . . . we might win?"

He leaned and touched his forehead to hers. "Yeah," he said softly. "Yeah."

Chapter Twenty-One

December 25, 2005

"Santa Claus was here!" Little girl lips pressed against Reesie's ears in what Aunt Tish called a "stage whisper," which meant it wasn't a whisper at all.

"Jazz, the sun isn't up yet!" Reesie mumbled. But her cousin rushed to the window and yanked the blinds open. Reesie pulled the covers over her head, wishing that there had been some other sleeping arrangement besides sharing a room with a kindergartener.

It felt like she'd just gone to bed. After staying up till all hours baking with Mom and Aunt Tish, she'd helped Uncle Teddy, Junior, and Orlando assemble both a bike and a tricycle with Japanese directions. In between, they'd played a rowdy Monopoly game and acted as judges to Daddy and Jimmy's oyster stuffing cook-off.

"Pleeeese! Reesie, pleeeese!" Jazz threw Reesie's covers off. Reesie moaned. Then she remembered how she used to do the same to Junior, practically dragging him out of bed on Christmas Day.

"Okay, okay." She blinked her sleepiness away and looked at herself in Jazz's pink princess mirror. Her hair was wild—she'd been too tired to wrap it with a scarf. Orlando couldn't see her this way! She grabbed Jazz's hairbrush.

"Come on!" Jazz was pulling at her. "You're already pretty!"

"Thanks, Jazzy." Reesie pulled jeans on with the oversize T-shirt she'd slept in. She could hear little Jason shouting downstairs already, and Uncle Teddy's good-natured grumbling.

At the foot of the stairs, Jazz caught sight of the tree and forgot all about Reesie. Reesie dropped to sit on the bottom step, taking everything in.

Jimmy, wearing a loud red velour robe, shouted names as he scooped boxes from underneath the Christmas tree, each time causing it to shudder dangerously. Junior was showing Jason how to set up his train set; Mama and Aunt Tish were laughing over how they'd gotten each other the same scarf.

Reesie hugged her knees. She hadn't expected that

everything would be so *normal*, but she didn't want it any other way.

"Merry, merry, baby girl!" Daddy ruffled her hair through the stair rail as he came from the kitchen with a mug of strong coffee and chicory. Reesie inhaled deeply. Yes, this was normal.

"Same to you, Daddy!" She jumped up to kiss him on the cheek, and bounced into the living room looking for Orlando.

"Hey, Merry Christmas, Peanut Butter." He was behind her.

She turned in surprise and grinned, thinking of Dré. She'd never noticed before how much they looked alike. Orlando pushed a clumsily wrapped package at her.

"Wow, thanks!"

"Well, I hope you have a gift for him too!" Daddy raised his eyebrows and passed by them.

Reesie shook herself. "Uh, yes! Course I do, Daddy!"

"Wait. Open yours first," Orlando said. He leaned against the wall, watching her. She was strangely aware that everyone else was watching her now too.

Reesie tore open the paper with one rip—she'd never been a careful gift opener.

There was a folded length of bright purple cotton fabric. Her mouth dropped open, and she looked up at

Orlando as if seeing him for the first time. His face lit up.

"I was thinking, you know, you're a designer, and all your—what you call it? Your *stash* was underwater!" He was talking fast. "And—and I know your favorite color is purple. You got purple shirts and a purple backpack and—"

Reesie dropped the fabric and threw her arms around his neck.

"Thank you! Thank you!" she said.

The family clapped as if they were in a TV show audience. Reesie let go of Orlando.

"Okay, y'all. Now you've embarrassed me in front of my boyfriend."

"Oohh! Boyfriend?" Uncle Teddy teased.

"What?" Junior said.

"When did this happen?" Mama asked.

"Somewhere around second grade, I think." Aunt Tish winked at Reesie, and Reesie wondered how aunts managed to remember every silly little detail you ever told them.

"Jimmy, you'd better keep this boy in line, now," Daddy said.

Orlando ran his hand over his hair. "Mr. Reesie's Dad," he said with a straight face, "is this okay with you?"

"I'm not the one to ask, Mr. Knight. It's got to be okay with Teresa."

Orlando blew a sigh of relief, and Reesie picked up her fabric, holding it tight as she went to search for his gift. It wasn't much, only a New York Yankees shirt, but she knew he'd wear it.

"Do you spell Orlando with an O?" Jazz asked, holding up the right package.

"Yeah, thanks!" Reesie said. And then Uncle Teddy rolled in the bikes, and high-pitched squeals and riding lessons took over.

"Reesie?" Aunt Tish was holding a gift bag. "Here's another one for you."

Reesie tipped around toys and stepped over boxes to get across the room. There was something heavy in the bag. Reesie lifted out the yellow tissue paper and saw a book. She looked at her aunt for a moment, then into the bag again.

"*Woman Everlasting*! Thank you so much!"

Aunt Tish hugged her tightly. "It was out of print, but I lucked out yesterday at that bookstore I know in New York. I thought you'd like to have it."

"Yes," Reesie said. "I—this Christmas—is the best I ever had."

Aunt Tish nodded. "Life can surprise you, kid.

Katrina was one of the bad surprises. But then those are the ones that make the good surprises so sweet."

A few hours later, once the feast was eaten, kids were calmed, and a football game was blasting in surround sound, Reesie and Orlando tried to sneak out of the house. She really wanted him to meet Dadi. Unfortunately, Orlando's struggle with a pair of Uncle Ted's snow boots slowed them down, and Reesie's mother materialized at the top of the stairs before they got to the door.

"Hey!" she said pleasantly. "Where are you two going at this hour on Christmas Day?"

"Mom, it's only five o'clock!" Reesie tried not to whine. The day had been wonderful so far, and she didn't want to ruin it.

"It's already dark, though."

"We're only walking up the street. The diner is open. I'm introducing Orlando to Dadi."

"Ah. The old friend meets the new." Her mother twisted her wrist to look at her watch. "Be back by seven."

Orlando straightened up, grinned, and saluted. "Yes, ma'am, Mrs. Sergeant Reesie's—"

Reesie jerked him out the door. Even after it was shut, they could hear her mother laughing. They held hands while tromping through the snow. It was almost too cold to speak, but Orlando managed. He filled her in on Jimmy's stubborn search for a new space to open up Blue Moon Two, on who was back in town and who was still MIA. He told her how both Dré and Eritrea had found work and an apartment uptown.

"Okay, so when are *you* coming back to New Orleans?" he asked.

"Spring break—April."

"I mean, for good."

They rounded the corner onto busy Bloomfield Avenue, and the glare of the streetlights and headlights made the new snow so bright that it almost seemed like daytime. Reesie looked over at Orlando and realized that she actually had to look up. He'd grown at least two inches taller since August.

"Depends on my mom," she said.

They stopped at the traffic light across the street from the Silver Diner. Reesie could see Felicidad watching from inside. She raised her arm to wave furiously. Dadi waved back, and it looked like she was saying, *Nice!*

"Yeah, you're right!" Reesie said under her breath as she ran across the wide street with Orlando Knight beside her.

PART FOUR

Finding Someplace

Chapter Twenty-Two

Reesie had never liked airplane takeoffs or landings. She closed her eyes, gripped the armrests, and pressed herself back against the seat, waiting for that odd sensation of lifting into the air. This time both her stomach and her knees were shaky, and she wasn't sure that flying again was the reason.

"Are you all right?" her mother whispered from the next seat.

"I don't know," Reesie said, looking out the window instead of at her mother. The plane was still climbing, but the winding ribbons of New Jersey highways were hardly visible anymore through the wispy clouds. In a few hours they'd land in Baton Rouge to spend the night with Parraine and Tee Charmaine. Tomorrow they'd drive into New Orleans.

"I'm not sure either," Mom said. She took off her reading glasses and dropped them onto the stack of folders in her lap.

Reesie knew the folders held letters and e-mails between her parents and FEMA, the government office that was supposed to help people during disasters. Reesie also knew from listening in on her parents' phone conversations that FEMA seemed to want proof of what people owned—before they would help—and every bit of the Boone proof had been snatched at the Superdome.

Reesie swallowed. These days she was getting better at fighting her fears and feelings of responsibility for what happened; still, she shifted uncomfortably. Mom noticed and quickly shoved the papers down into the tote bag between her feet.

"You know, when my parents died in that car accident, I was afraid nothing would ever feel normal again. Nothing would *be* normal again."

Reesie wondered what made her mother bring that awful subject up. Aunt Tish had been only seven or eight, her mother thirteen. They were visiting an aunt, and their parents were coming to pick them up. It was the visit that never ended.

"In Miss Martine's attic I thought some crazy stuff," Reesie said. "I wondered how anybody could go on if they lost everything."

Mom nodded.

"And I just realized—you did that, Mom. You went through something huge, something tragic!" Reesie lowered her voice. "It's like . . . walking through the world when nothing is real but you, right?"

"Right." Mom played with the heart necklace, which she hadn't taken off since Christmas. "But I put one foot in front of the other and made it to nursing school in New Orleans, and met your dad." She laughed a little. "He made things real, all right! We got married, had Junior, had you. I woke up one day and looked around, and said to myself: 'This is normal!'"

"That's what 'new normal' means. I get it."

Mom tilted her head and looked at Reesie hard. "But deep down I lived every day afraid that I would lose everything again."

Reesie had never known her mother to be timid, or to shy away from anything. She was a surgical nurse! Then the scene at the motel flashed into Reesie's memory.

"Mom—you thought you wouldn't find me, didn't you?"

Her mother took a deep breath. "When I heard about the flooding and the levees breaking? I lost it. I couldn't find my husband. I didn't know what happened to my daughter. We had coworkers who disappeared. Every hour I got madder, mad as hell at New Orleans, and at your father for making me love it."

"Wow." Reesie had to take a minute to wrap her head around this conversation. This wasn't kid stuff, hearing what went on between her parents. But then, she hadn't felt like a kid for the last eight months. Inside her there had been an almost constant tug-of-war between hope and fear about going back.

"Mom?"

"Yes, baby?"

"We're moving back for good when school is out, right?"

Her mother nodded slowly. "I promised your dad."

Reesie hoped she might one day be as strong as Jeannie Boone. She turned to the window again. Now the plane was cruising along a thick white carpet of clouds, and as far as she could see, the sky was a bright and perfect blue. *But life's not perfect*, she thought.

She put her headphones on and zoned out for the rest of the flight.

At baggage claim Reesie stood on her toes to scan for Parraine's shining bald head.

"Hey, girls!" Tee Charmaine's voice rang from two luggage carousels away. Reesie turned in her direction and ran.

"Yeah!" Parraine crooned. "The Boones are back on home ground!" He caught Reesie first, swinging her into the air like her father always did.

"Well, how much did you grow?" Tee Charmaine was all of about five feet tall, and Reesie had passed that mark before her birthday. She laughed. Tee Charmaine could always make her laugh.

"Didn't she?" Mom was smiling proudly.

"Did you sew that skirt?" Tee Charmaine asked.

Reesie looked down at the simple wrap skirt she'd made from the fabric Orlando had given her. "Yes." She smiled. "But I'm still getting used to Aunt Tish's sewing machine."

"Nice job!" Tee Charmaine said.

"You still playin' ball up there in New Jersey?" Parraine asked over his shoulder, lifting one of their ridiculously large suitcases off the revolving rack.

"Softball? Nahh." Reesie shrugged. She hadn't thought about softball in a long time. "Things change," she said. He seemed to skip a beat, staring at her. *That's funny*, Reesie thought. Tee Charmaine could see that she'd changed outside, but couldn't Parraine see that she must've changed inside, too?

Reesie's phone vibrated, and she answered it.

"You landed?" Orlando asked. She had begun to like hearing his voice so often, her cell phone bill was dangerously close to becoming an issue.

"Yeah. We'll be in New Orleans tomorrow," she said.

"Let me know when you hit the city, and I'll come by your house. Remember, I said, 'It's not pretty,' okay?"

"I remember. See you."

"Later." When she looked up, her mother and aunt had strolled ahead, but Parraine was looking at her suspiciously.

"What was all that?" he asked. "Who're you gonna see?"

"It was nothing, Parraine," she said, clicking up the handle on her rolling bag. "I heard you got a new ride!" Parraine couldn't resist talking cars. Tee Charmaine hated it, so it was Reesie and Parraine in the front seats of the still new-smelling Chrysler.

Soon they were in familiar territory. The low brick ranch houses and big old trees lining the streets looked exactly the way they had nearly a year ago. Inside, Reesie wandered slowly through the rooms, pausing to look at framed photos of her cousin Angela, grown and moved away; of Ma Maw; of the grandfather she'd never met. A shiver went through her when she picked up one that was a twin to a photo that had been in her own house, frame and all. It was the one of Daddy getting his promotion. She'd had it in the backpack.

Her aunt and uncle's house smelled of floor wax and spices and Tee Charmaine's floral perfume. Like always.

Reesie should have felt comfortable. They sat around in the kitchen and laughed and remembered old family times. When exhaustion made her eyelids droop and her entire body feel like lead, she crashed across the bed in Angela's old room. Like always.

She was walking down her street on that August day, talking on her cell to Orlando. Waving at Miss Martine. Feeling a drop on her forehead. When she wiped it, sand flung from her fingers. She dropped her phone and looked around. She was surrounded by sand. Bright white sand that shifted and

drifted into hot waves. The sun was burning the top of her bare head. She tried to yell for help, but no sounds came out of her throat. She was in a desert, alone.

Reesie sat upright. It was dark. Her heart was pounding. Tomorrow wouldn't be like always.

Chapter Twenty-Three

"I got a surprise for my goddaughter!" Parraine announced at the breakfast table. Reesie had just eaten a mouthful of hot grits, so she grabbed her glass of juice to wash it down.

"Surprise?" She almost choked. Tee Charmaine had a puzzled expression, and Mom avoided eye contact with her by reading a newspaper. Parraine slid a scrap of yellow notebook paper across the table. Reesie frowned at the scrawled address. She had no idea what—or where—it was. Parraine took a swig of coffee and stood.

"Yeah, surprise. You didn't get too grown for those up in New Jersey, did you?"

"Nooo . . ." Reesie was still a little brain-cloudy from her dream, so she couldn't guess what her uncle had up his sleeve.

"Go on and finish eating, Reesie. We have a stop to make before we get on the road to New Orleans!"

Reesie hurried through the rest of her meal, brushed her teeth, and met her uncle at the car. Mom and Tee Charmaine were whispering and smiling mysteriously on the porch as Parraine drove off.

"Okay, I can't stand it," Reesie said, uncrumpling the address. "Where are we going?"

"You can't figure it out?" Parraine laughed.

Reesie racked her brain. She hadn't been to many places in Baton Rouge before, besides her uncle's house, their church, Angela's old high school. But they'd left the neighborhood behind and were heading toward some kind of hospital complex.

"Wait!" Reesie slapped the dashboard. "Wait!"

"Yeah?" Parraine said. "You got it?"

Reesie leaned her head back on the seat. "Miss Martine."

It wasn't exactly a hospital; it was more like a special apartment building for older people. When they walked in, there was a desk with a security guard, where Parraine had to check in. The guard told them to wait in the lobby, and he motioned to the left, past a bank of elevators.

The large living-room-like space was empty. Through

the wall of glass windows at the back Reesie saw people sitting or walking in what looked like a flower garden.

The elevator doors swished open. Reesie jumped up.

"Miss Martine!"

"Well, Teresa!" Miss Martine was a little thinner and moved a little slower, but she had on a curly silver beehive wig, and wore new purple glasses—cat-eye, of course.

"I'm so glad you're all right!" Reesie couldn't stop grinning. "I was so worried when we had to leave you—"

Miss Martine settled herself on one of the fluffy couches, and Reesie sat beside her. Miss Martine patted Reesie's knee.

"You were so brave. I know how that water must have terrified you, after that swimming pool scare you had!"

"How"—Reesie looked at Parraine, but he shook his head—"how did you know?" she finished.

Miss Martine smiled. "Your grandmother and I had many cups of tea together, Teresa. Edith was a wonderful, strong woman. You are her legacy."

"I am?" Reesie turned the idea over in her mind. Daddy had called their house a legacy in the heated argument. Was this how life worked as you grew up—everything got connected?

"Yeah, you are," Parraine said so low that Reesie almost didn't hear. She wasn't sure if she was supposed to.

❧

Parraine drove into New Orleans on Interstate 10, the same route he'd tried to take on that August day so long ago. It was midafternoon, and traffic seemed light as they passed through Metairie, a suburb right outside of the city.

Reesie sat in the backseat with her headphones plugged into her ears and her face so close to the window that her nose touched the glass. Over the months she had thought often about coming back, and now that small fear she'd had when she got on the plane had managed to grow.

Being in New Jersey for so long, without her friends or anything familiar, had almost convinced her that Katrina must have happened in some other place, some other New Orleans, in an alternate universe. But Miss Martine had been reality. What Reesie was about to face was reality, and she really wasn't prepared at all. Her hands were clenched so tightly around her iPod that its metal casing dug into her palms. Her heart beat fast right along with the house music.

Everywhere she looked she saw the trail the hurricane had left behind. Many of the warehouses and industrial buildings that lined the highway were stripped down to their wood and metal skeletons. Huge trees lay with their roots clawing the air, some on top of fences and cars—and houses. This damage was clearly caused by wind—hurricane-force winds, not water. She tried to relax.

As I-10 curved into the city, it curled around the Superdome. All their heads turned to take in the beautiful round shape and the tiny specks of the workers on top of it, repairing the holes where Katrina had ripped away the roofing and poured herself inside. Reesie exhaled, and only then realized that she'd been holding her breath.

Parraine got off the highway, first cruising along Canal Street as if they were tourists. Reesie counted store after store with windows boarded, or plastered with big signs saying CLOSED. As they neared the French Quarter there were real tourists wandering the sidewalks, and sun glinted off the iron balconies and the clean cobbled streets. But Reesie kept thinking of the purple sneakers that she'd never gotten to wear, of Ayanna and herself eating beignets, laughing at the notion of a killer hurricane. She shivered.

"Too much air conditioning?" Tee Charmaine asked loudly from the front.

"No!" Reesie said in a sharp voice. "I'm fine, thanks," she quickly added.

Two things stood out from the rest of the strangeness winding across town through the Sixth and Seventh Wards. One, she thought must be her imagination—a shadowy dark line that ran straight across every house, garage, and even some of the stranded cars in sight. She blinked, but as they continued driving, the line still seemed to be there. The other weird thing was a fluorescent orange *X* that was spray-painted prominently on almost all of the houses. There were numbers around the sides of the *X*s. She couldn't figure it out.

"Parraine? What's with those orange *X*s?" she asked, dropping one earbud. He glanced at her in the rearview mirror.

"Means they went in there, checking for people," he said. "There're numbers for survivors, and zeroes if they didn't find anybody, depends on where the number is."

"But some of them have more than two numbers."

Her mother touched her arm gently. "There's a number for people who didn't make it, baby."

Reesie frowned. *Which is which?* She wanted to know, but didn't ask. She pushed her earbud back in. *Tic-tac-toe for the dead*, she thought. She could never play that game again. She turned away, just in time to spot the green-and-white ST. CLAUDE BRIDGE sign.

In the middle of the bridge she raised her head to look

out across the Ninth Ward. The destruction was every-where, making the neighborhood almost unrecognizable.

And then Parraine exited off the ramp the boats had rowed up on, the day someone reached from these very rails and touched her fingers.

She opened the window to breathe in New Orleans air. It smelled of dampness and dirt. The remains of houses lay in pieces, scattered planks of wood and Sheetrock and sections of siding were piled everywhere. Reesie blinked. Tossed among the ruins were human things—curtains and clothes, broken furniture and appliances.

Reesie was completely disoriented; so few buildings were left standing, and there were no street signs in sight. The jagged and broken trees seemed dead. Cars were crushed underneath collapsed garages or carports.

"Can't go any farther," she heard Parraine say, and Reesie looked frantically around for their house as he pulled to the right and stopped. What she saw were roof-tops, two of them, blocking the mud-caked street in front of the car.

"So many lives just floated away," her mother said, slowly stepping out of the car.

And Reesie understood, for the first time, the truth of that. Entire houses had washed away, along with the belongings of the families who'd lived in them. Along with some of the people who'd lived in them.

She swallowed, finding that there was a lump in her throat. She had been so absorbed in her own pain and problems after Katrina that the bigness of the picture had never come clear. Had she hidden from all this on purpose, she wondered? She couldn't hide anymore. Reesie opened her door. The bottoms of her feet tingled when they touched the ground.

The adults were talking a lot about the damage now.

"Some houses got washed right off their foundations," Parraine was saying as they passed a huge yellow bulldozer parked atop a mound of rubble. "The city is all through here, tearing down buildings before they fall down. They'll be back to clear those roofs out of the street too."

"I guess we were lucky," her mother said. Parraine didn't say anything.

"There are some homes in decent shape over on Deslondes," Tee Charmaine said. She stepped around a shattered window lying on the ground that still had curtains attached.

"Yeah," said Parraine. "When I came by here the other week, Lloyd and I saw Elizabeth Smith over there. One of her boys is working in her house, but she's the only one back in that block."

"She's in her house?" Mom asked.

Parraine shook his head. "Heck, no! No power back over there yet, and the water is still funky."

"Unbelievable," Mom murmured.

Reesie looked to her left and saw a sturdy concrete porch and its three steps with iron rails . . . with no house attached. She knew that porch. She didn't know the name of the family who lived there, but she had always seen a man sitting there when she passed by. She wondered where that man was.

All at once she was hit with the same out-of-body feeling that she'd had only once before in her life; she was saddened beyond tears and sick to her stomach, and could hardly breathe. When Ma Maw died, she'd felt this way.

The house with the porch was on Reynes Street. Slowly, Reesie got her bearings. One block farther, then a left . . . She was ahead of her mother, hurrying around a truck whose hood was tiled with dried mud, and a couple of downed trees.

Dauphine Street. Her street.

Chapter Twenty-Four

There was the neat redbrick house with white iron window gates. The electrical pole near the curb looked as though its top half had been chewed off, and it was leaning at a crazy angle over a heap of junk. Reesie caught sight of a cream-and-red stripe that she recognized. It was a section of wallpaper from their kitchen. She practically jumped back, bumping the vehicle sitting in the driveway. She turned to stare at the blue Honda. It was her uncle's old car.

Of course, she thought. Parraine would have given his car to Daddy, because both his and Mom's must be in a scrapyard somewhere. She stepped carefully over some cables into what had been their front yard, and felt her mother's hand slip into hers.

"Here we go," Mom whispered.

"How're you doing?" Reesie asked, thinking of their conversation on the plane. Her mother only had a chance to nod before the door popped open.

"Jeannie! Reesie!" Daddy wrapped them both up in his arms there on the stoop. Reesie peeked inside over his shoulder.

"Dang . . . ," she muttered. Neither of her parents corrected her. They followed her inside.

They were standing in the midst of bare bones—even the walls between the rooms were gone. Reesie could see straight through this, the used-to-be living room, to the nonexistent hallway, to the weirdly unfamiliar space that should have been her bedroom.

She tasted the tears that had begun to run down her cheeks, but she didn't bother to wipe them. Her emotions were oddly disconnected: they'd lost something they couldn't replace, yes. But was she devastated? No. For a minute Reesie thought the old guilt might kick in again. It didn't. *Legacy*, Daddy had said. *Legacy*, Miss Martine had said.

"Oh . . . Lloyd!" Mom's words echoed, and Reesie winced at the sound. Her parents seemed small as they stood huddled together in the middle of the empty space. She couldn't look at them.

The smell of wet wood was so strong that she reached out to one of the exposed beams. It was—still—soft and damp to her touch. How could that be, months after the flood?

"Daddy?"

Her father sighed. *How hard it must have been for him!* Reesie thought.

"Listen." He was clearly speaking more to her mother than to her, so she stayed where she was, in the hallway that wasn't.

"We can't save the house." His words dropped like rocks.

"But, Lloyd! The insurance—I've been going over the papers, and—"

"No, Jeannie. No." Daddy shook his head and walked away toward the back of the house as if he couldn't face them. Reesie instinctively moved closer, as did her mother.

"Pete and I had an engineer come out. The place is structurally unsound. And the money FEMA is offering us, even with the insurance payout, won't be enough to rebuild from scratch."

"Couldn't you use my college money?" Reesie heard herself asking. Her father turned with his shoulders slumped, and pain was written all over his face. But he managed a smile.

"No, I cannot, Reesie Bear. Your grandmother would roll in her grave if I put this collection of brick and wood over you and your brother getting an education. It wasn't about the house for her; it was about me and Pete being better off."

"Your mother was right, as always," Mom said firmly. "But this, Lloyd, is about the kids as much as it's about us, isn't it? We won't give up on this. So, we'll find a rental, and we'll start saving."

Reesie watched her father's shoulders snap to attention. Superman was weakened, but he hadn't given in.

"Jeannie. This ride isn't going to be easy from here on. Are you sure, now?"

"I'm sure."

Reesie had the feeling that her parents had forgotten that she was there. She quietly eased to the door and out. Blinking in the sun, she shaded her eyes. There was no sign of Parraine and Tee Charmaine, but she only thought of them for a moment before her phone buzzed. She looked at the screen: Orlando.

"Peanut Butter! How come you didn't call me? Y'all already there?"

"Yeah. Sorry. I—"

"I'm not mad at you. It's rough, right? You okay?"

Reesie smiled. "Yeah."

"That's what I'm talkin' about! Hey, I'm in the car with Tree and Dré. They're gonna bring me by your house, and then they want to have ya'll come by and eat. Tell your mama."

"I will," Reesie said. "See you."

"Sooner than you think!" Orlando laughed, clicking off.

Reesie slipped her phone into the backpack slung over her shoulder. She was still smiling, even as she looked across the twisted landscape in front of her. She shoved her hands into her pockets and walked up the street in the direction of Miss Martine's, kicking dust with the toes of her sneakers.

She was alone, just like in her last dream. The layers of dried mud covered the blacktop completely, so it looked like the road had never been paved—or as if there was no road at all. There were none of the noises of living around her, no dogs barking or birds and cicadas calling from trees. It was a type of desert, she thought as she went on.

Miss Martine's house was gone. Even the lot had been

cleared down to the cinder block foundation. Only Dré's brick shed was still standing where it had been, with its door shut tight and the little window's panes unbroken. Something green caught Reesie's eye.

At one edge of the house's foundation, near what would have been the back door, were the remains of a little flower bed marked by a row of bricks embedded halfway into the ground. Green spring grass had come up. And unfurling out of that grass were the slender stems of "elephant ears"—Miss Martine called them caladiums.

Reesie whipped out her phone and stooped close to take a picture of them. *That bright green against red brick would make a great painting*, she thought.

And why, she wondered as she straightened up, *do I have to think of this nothingness as the end of* anything?

On the spot, she did a 360-degree turn to take in everything her eyes could see. It was bleak, it was ugly. She snapped a picture. Far down the street she could see a truck pull up at a lopsided house. People got out and began unloading sheets of plywood. She snapped again.

Nothing was the same, Orlando had said. This was new normal, and she was new normal Reesie. She was finished with nightmares and feeling afraid for her family and herself. She was finished with feeling afraid about losing old friends and making new ones.

Katrina could not win this fight. Teresa Arielle Boone would not let her. It *was* going to be hard, but she would keep on going, just like her parents and her friends were doing. Just like New Orleans was doing.

She walked back to the shed and squatted in front of the red door. The paint was peeling, and the wood was buckled. She pushed against it, but the lock held. She twisted her body into a sitting position and opened her backpack.

First she took out her phone and texted Orlando to tell him where she was. Then she dug deeper into the bag and pulled out *Woman Everlasting*.

It was odd, but just right, that she hadn't taken the time before now to actually read any of it; she felt trembly inside again as she leafed through the yellowed pages.

There it was. The poem titled "Finding Someplace."

She looked up quickly, then reminded herself that no one was there to hear her reading out loud. And to her surprise she discovered that she really wouldn't care if anyone did. Reesie tilted the book away from the mid-day glare.

the mat says
welcome, *but*
my heart reads:
'enter here,
and be loved.'
and yes, there's always
another dream
to chase, or
friend to follow,
always
one
more
photo to take
before returning
before embracing
the old life
that's fading
in the brightness of
now; but let me tell you:

find someplace

get yourself somewhere
that you can always

enter,
knowing
you will
be
loved.

Reesie closed the book and got up stiffly, brushing dust off herself. She started to put the book away but decided not to: she wanted to show her parents and Eritrea and Dré—and Orlando. She wanted to explain to them how well she understood Miss Martine's words. She'd learned a lot about the people in her life since that day in the attic, and a lot about herself.

She'd found her *someplace*—by the hardest, as Miss Martine would say—and the funny thing was: it wasn't even a place. It was the people who'd made her feel strong, even when she wasn't. It was the people who felt like family, even when they weren't. Reesie smiled to herself. She could carry her *someplace* around with her always now, because it was inside her heart.

AUTHOR'S NOTE

We ride through the Lower Ninth Ward early on New Year's Eve, along the real streets portrayed in Reesie Boone's story. Her world is based on the facts of this world, one of the many New Orleans neighborhoods swallowed up by floodwaters during Hurricane Katrina back in 2005.

As this novel ends, Reesie sees and experiences some new beginnings in her life, yet much is left unfinished.

This is the truth of the Ninth Ward even today. On my aunt's street, some houses remain boarded up and some lots are empty because the houses were so damaged they had to be torn down. But many homes have been rebuilt. Sun bounces off new windows. Newness feels like it's everywhere inside my aunt's renovated house: walls, cabinets, appliances, towels, and even dishes have been replaced.

After our visit, my aunt walks us out to the front porch. Children wave to her and shout to each other as they ride the shiny new bikes they got for Christmas. As we drive away, the pavement seems rough and hard for the car to navigate, but we keep going.

I wonder if the families who made this community come alive again have had the same journey. Some, like the fictional Boone family, have returned and worked for years to rebuild their homes and their lives here. It's been rough. It's been hard. Their lives are not exactly the same, but they keep going.

Ten years ago, New Orleans—and the Ninth Ward— was someplace lost. Like Reesie Boone, it seems this city has discovered where its true strength lies: not in its beautiful buildings, or its great music and food, or even in its ability to come back from such a disaster, but in the people who love it.

—DLP

ACKNOWLEDGMENTS

Special thanks to Ottyle, Otlisha, Yanada, Jada, my Cherokee Street cousins, all of my East Coast friends for their generosity, and to Christy and Amy for their incredible patience!

GOFISH

DENISE LEWIS PATRICK

What was your inspiration for *Finding Someplace*?
As I watch disasters unfold in the news, I think most people so easily forget events and situations that don't directly affect them. But for the families and communities that live through these disasters, life is changed forever. I wanted to create characters who help readers understand what that experience is like. This book is about Hurricane Katrina and New Orleans, but the feelings and reactions the characters have could happen as a result of other situations, anywhere.

Do you have a personal connection to New Orleans?
Definitely. My father was born and grew up there. I spent a good part of my childhood visiting my grandparents, aunts, uncles, and cousins in the city. I have great memories of things like learning to roller skate on the sidewalks of the Seventh Ward, taking the streetcars, and eating big square doughnuts called beignets.

What do you want readers to remember about Reesie's story?
I want readers to come away from this story feeling, as Reesie does, that Reesie started out as a girl in her own little world, and grew through this intense time to see herself as a

young woman who is stronger inside than she thought she was. She also realizes how fortunate she is to be surrounded and supported by strong family, friends, and community.

What did you want to be when you grew up?
Honestly, I didn't think much about that when I was very young. I was spending my time reading and drawing cartoons and fooling around learning to use my mother's sewing machine. Later, I considered becoming a doctor, or even a lawyer—but what I really wanted to do was write. It wasn't until I was a teenager that I realized I might actually want to make a career out of writing.

What's your favorite childhood memory?
Hanging around the older women in my family. I do remember sitting in my New Orleans grandmother's kitchen in my pink high chair, listening to the radio with her while she drank coffee. I walked around my aunt Mable's yard with her, learning about gardening, and I absolutely loved being with my aunts and their friends, because they were teenagers when I was a little girl, and being with them made me feel grown-up.

What book is on your nightstand now?
Oh, there's a stack. I have *Wicked* by Gregory Maguire, which I still haven't read; *Mockingjay* by Suzanne Collins; a poetry anthology; and a book for adults by Madeleine L'Engle called *Walking on Water.* (I'm a big *A Wrinkle in Time* fan.) And, of course, the first copy of *Finding Someplace* that I got from my publisher.

If you could travel in time, where would you go and what would you do?
I don't know about traveling back in time, but if it didn't take so long, I'd really like to go into space. I think having a view of

the earth and planets and stars would be so awesome that I would think differently about everything in my life when I got back.

What's the best advice you have ever received about writing?

Wow. I didn't meet other writers until I became one myself. It was then that I also began to read what other writers said about this career. But I think the best advice is what I've learned, and what I tell young would-be writers: Read! Read whatever, whenever you can. I regret now that I don't have more hours in each day to read all the books I want to.

Who is your favorite fictional character?

Mrs. Weasley from the Harry Potter series. She welcomes Harry into her family as if he were one of her own, she makes great soup, and she gives great hugs and smiles. But her kids discover that she has this other life as a member of the Order of the Phoenix. She isn't afraid to fight for what's right.

What do you consider to be your greatest accomplishment?

Raising my four sons to become young men who anyone would be proud of, as their parents are.